"*Brenner and God* is one of the cleverest—and most thoroughly enjoyable—mysteries that I've read in a long time. Wolf Haas is the real deal, and his arrival on the American book scene is long overdue." **—CARL HIAASEN, AUTHOR OF *SICK PUPPY***

"A meticulously plotted, dark, and often very funny ride."
—THE MILLIONS

"*Brenner and God* is a humdinger ... a sockdollager of an action yarn, revealed via the smart-ass, self-effacing narrative voice that's a sort of trademark of author Wolf Haas." **—THE AUSTIN CHRONICLE**

"[A] superb translation of one of Austria's finest crime novels ... Haas never loses the thread of investigation, even as he introduces off-beat characters and a very complex plot ... This is the first of the Brenner novels in English. We can only hope for more, soon."
—THE GLOBE AND MAIL (TORONTO)

"Even as Haas darkens the mood of this sly and entertaining novel, he maintains its sardonically irreverent tone."
—THE BARNES & NOBLE REVIEW

"A pacey and gripping read." **—EURO CRIME**

"A gleaming gem of a novel." **—CRIMESPREE MAGAZINE**

"[From] the insanely talented and clever Wolf Haas ... A satirical and cynical criticism of Austrian and German society is very much a part of the plot, just as Chandler, Hammett and the other great American hard-boiled writers had an indictment of our society at heart." **—THE DIRTY LOWDOWN**

"Simon Brenner has been brilliantly brought to life by Mr. Haas' subtle yet masterful prose, with just the right balance of dark humor ... Mr. Haas may not yet be a household name, this side of the Atlantic, but all that is about to change."

—NEW YORK JOURNAL OF BOOKS

"This quirkily funny kidnapping caper marks the first appearance in English of underdog sleuth Simon Brenner ... Austrian author Haas brings a wry sense of humor ... American readers will look forward to seeing more of Herr Simon." **—PUBLISHERS WEEKLY**

"One of Germany's most loved thriller writers: he's celebrated by the literary critics and venerated by the readers." **—DER SPIEGEL**

"This is great art, great fun." **—GERMANY RADIO**

PRAISE FOR *THE BONE MAN*

"Darkly comic ... American mystery fans should enjoy Haas's quirky, digressive storytelling style." **—PUBLISHERS WEEKLY**

"It's a novel that leaves you laughing even as you work to solve the mystery." **—THE GLOBE AND MAIL (TORONTO)**

"A brilliant book ... Already among the greats of mystery fiction." **—BOOK DEVIL**

"The most original figure here is the narrator, who hovers above the action with matter-of-fact detachment, ever alert for moments when he can swoop down and set you straight about what's going on or change the subject entirely." **—KIRKUS**

WOLF HAAS was born in 1960 in the Austrian province of Salzburg. He is the author of seven books in the bestselling Brenner mystery series, three of which have been adapted into major German-language films by director Wolfgang Murnberger. Among other prizes, the books in the series have been awarded the German Thriller Prize and the 2004 Literature Prize from the city of Vienna. Haas lives in Vienna.

ANNIE JANUSCH is the translator of the Art of the Novella series edition of Heinrich von Kleist's *The Duel*, as well Wolf Haas' *Brenner and God* and *The Bone Man*.

D.

RESURRECTION

WOLF HAAS

HAAS

RESURRECTION

TRANSLATED BY ANNIE JANUSCH

 MELVILLE HOUSE
BROOKLYN · LONDON | MELVILLE
INTERNATIONAL
CRIME

MELVILLE INTERNATIONAL CRIME

RESURRECTION

First published in Germany as *Auferstehung der Toten*

Copyright © 1996 by Rowohlt Taschenbuch
Verlag GmbH, Reinbek bei Hamburg

Translation copyright © 2013 by Annie Janusch

First Melville House Printing: January 2014

Melville House Publishing   8 Blackstock Mews
145 Plymouth Street   and   Islington
Brooklyn, NY 11201   London N4 2BT

mhpbooks.com   facebook.com/mhpbooks   @melvillehouse

Library of Congress Cataloging-in-Publication Data

Haas, Wolf, author.
  [Auferstehung der Toten. English]
  Resurrection / Wolf Haas ; translated by Annie Janusch.
    pages   cm. — (Melville International Crime)
  ISBN 978-1-61219-270-3 (pbk.)
  ISBN 978-1-61219-271-0 (ebook)
    1. Ex–police officers—Austria—Fiction.   2. Private
investigators—Austria—Fiction.   3. Murder—Investigation—
Austria—Fiction.   4. Mystery fiction.   5. Suspense fiction.   I.
Janusch, Annie, translator.   II. Title.
  PT2708.A17A9413 2014
  833'.92—dc23

                           2013044737

Manufactured in the United States of America
1 3 5 7 9 10 8 6 4 2

The translation of this book was supported by the
Austrian Federal Ministry of Education, Arts, and Culture.

RESURRECTION

As far as America goes, Zell's a tiny speck. Middle of Europe somewhere. As far as Pinzgau's concerned, though, Zell's the capital of Pinzgau. Ten thousand inhabitants, thirty mountains over 3,000 meters high, fifty-eight ski lifts, one lake. And believe it or not. Last December, two Americans were killed in Zell. But for now, get a load of this.

After the war, it was the skiing that brought prosperity to Zell. Suddenly, snowfall meant money on the ground. But it goes without saying: you can't be too lazy to bend down and pick it up.

Take the lift operators, for instance. All day long they've got to watch out that nobody falls out of the lift. Day in, day out, thousands of skiers swooshing right past them. Nobody ever falls out of the lift usually, but if it should happen, not the end of the world, either. Lift operator's just got to go over to the emergency brake and turn the lift off. And no easy job. Looks easy, but it's not as easy as it looks. On account of the cold. Doesn't matter how good a thermal suit St. Nick brings you. Won't do you any good in the long run. That's why, throughout the land, you can recognize lift operators by their frostbit red noses. Enough to make you think, Those aren't lift operators at all, but secret clowns, making fun of the whole charade that's got them chasing all over the place in every kind of weather.

One lift operator, though, the people tell stories about him, Alois the Lift Operator, or Alois the Lift for short, how he used to sometimes let the local kids through for free. Well, on the morning of December twenty-second, after the longest night of the year, there was something else altogether that had him cursing. Not the crap-ass weather, even though the weather was crap-ass awful.

He rode in like he always did with Wörgötter in his snowcat to the Panorama Lift station in the valley. Wörgötter let him off, and he hopped out into the dawn and went straight to the lift cabin, and, like he did every morning, turned the radiator on first and then the radio.

And just like every morning, one of them little punks from the night before had left it dialed to Ö3, and of course, all Alois the Lift had to say about that was: "Ghetto music." So, there he is, turning the dial like he does every morning, nice and slowly to the left, because it was an old radio. A person who can turn a dial slower than Alois, well, not easy to find. You'd have thought he was defusing a bomb. And, on top of it all, Alois the Lift's got his little finger jutting out like some withered twig. On account of him cutting it with a circular saw when he was a kid.

So, he finally gets his station in. Where it's always the old times all the time. And good music. Half an hour ago,

Alois the Lift, sound asleep still. Now, he's happy just to be listening along over a Thermos of coffee to these old stories.

Take the snow, for instance. Time and again they dig up that story about how twenty or even just a few years ago, there used to be way more snow. Well, needless to say, Alois the Lift knows best: not a word of it true.

It was just the liftees and the innkeepers that started the rumor because, ordinarily, it was only every other or every third winter that there was snow during the Christmas holidays. And needless to say, the skiers, not exactly satisfied—saving up their money all year long up north in the Ruhr Valley just to sit around their hotel rooms.

Or else just to go swooshing over slopes that've only got a light dusting on them and ruining their new gear on their first day out. The gastronomes sure liked dishing up that story about the climate change. Because that's how people are—they cope much easier with some great calamity like the destruction of the earth than they do a minor misfortune like the destruction of their new skis.

And these days when you're a tourist someplace, you're just happy if a local talks to you. That's why every waiter and gas station attendant has got away with dishing up this story since, well, always, to the German and Dutch tourists, about how everything, but especially the snow, used to be way better. And they're just biding their time till January, because it'll definitely snow in January, so much that you won't even be able to ski on account of the avalanches.

But, this December, everything was different. There was

so much snow that Alois the Lift could barely see out of the operator's cabin where he'd just took a sip of Thermos-coffee. On the radio somebody was talking about the last time there was this much snow. Believe it or not: before the war.

As Alois the Lift walks out of the cabin—because he's got to get the chairlift going on the daily test run—he can still see Wörgötter's snowcat, barely making a dent in the snow. "White gold," they'd be saying in Zell. But Alois the Lift couldn't hear anything just then besides the noise from the snowcat and the chairlift starting up. He was two lifts away from the village—he couldn't even see the village, because he couldn't even see twenty meters in front of him in this heavy snowfall.

Alois the Lift couldn't see the snowcat anymore now, either, but then Wörgötter switched all eight of its lights on, and needless to say. All at once, all the slopes lit up, bright as day on this dark, dark morning after the longest night of the year.

The parcel that was slowly approaching on one of the lift seats, though. Alois the Lift couldn't fully make it out yet. Naturally he wondered how there could even be something on the seat. Every evening the lift goes on a quality-control run so that nothing gets left behind on a seat. It was the oldest chairlift in Zell, still a one-seater—didn't even have a double. But, for as long as Alois the Lift could remember—and he'd been working the lift the second-longest of anybody—there'd never been anything left on a seat in the morning.

"Those idiots!" Alois the Lift muttered, and he was

getting cold in the gusts of snow now, because every year, the parkas got better, but the wind just stang all the more.

"Those idiots didn't do a control run yesterday!"

Those idiots would be the same young liftees who were always switching the radio over to the "ghetto music." And as the massive parcel got closer, Alois the Lift's thoughts just turned darker and darker.

He had very good eyes, because he always protected them with those Carrera sunglasses that St. Nick had brought him some years ago. But the bundle was covered in such a thick coat of snow that he still couldn't make out with any certainty what it was. Even though it was only a few seats away from the station. Or at least that's how he told it, Alois the Lift, that night at the Rainerwirt.

"That's when I could tell that it wasn't just some empty case of beer from New Zealand, the ski disco, like I thought at first. But then," as Alois the Lift told it at the *Rainerwirt* on the twenty-second—and then, on the twenty-third, in nearly the same words, all over again at the *Hirschen*:

"But that's when I realized."

Forty years Alois the Lift had been stationed on the lift, and countless serious accidents had happened on the slopes in that time. Often enough Martin the helicopter had to come—twice somebody fell out of the chair. There'd actually been so many deaths that, over the years, they all ran together in Alois's mind.

Not to mention New Zealand's victims, who got crushed beneath the snowcat in the dark. See, the drunks fall down in the snow and then are too tired to get back up. And when you're drunk, the snow seems so warm to you. So they just lie there in the warm snow and get a little shut-eye. Next morning, all you can do is send the corpses back to Germany.

But a dead body in a lift seat on the morning line-check, well, Alois the Lift had never had that happen before.

"What in god's name!" Alois the Lift yelled out.

Now, you should know. For years, Alois had acted in his community theater troupe. The community theater troupe was founded in the mid-sixties by the tourism bureau. It goes without saying, though, billed to the tourists as some relic out of the Stone Age. This winter they put on *The Truth about Moser Gudrun*. A play in three acts, it said on the posters, by Silvia Soll. And among the actors listed on the posters, Alois the Lift came in third: "Alois Mitteregger (Alois the Lift)."

Alois the Lift was a real darling among community-theater-goers. But when he described the incident from the valley station at the Rainerwirt that night, well, community theater doesn't come close.

"What in god's name, I cried out," he cried out—and so loud that everybody in the whole bar could understand. "I switched that lift off as fast it'd go to Off. Even though it was obvious that there was nothing left to do. But when you're scared, you do it as fast as you can. Even if there's no point. Because, if, first thing in the morning, somebody's sitting on the lift, then he's been sitting there all night. Since we don't run it in between," Alois the Lift says.

"It gave me a scare, of course, so I brought the lift to a halt a.s.a.p. We've had first aid, you know, mouth-to-mouth.

But you'll be doing mouth-to-mouth a long time with fifteen centimeters of snow between you and the body. Even though it'd just started snowing that morning. Been a clear starry sky that night. I took the dog out after the eight o'clock movie, and it was clear. And when it's starry like that here, end of December, it's at least seven degrees in the dead of night," Alois the Lift says.

"Seven below," Alois the Lift says, and looks at his listeners just long enough for them to get a little nervous. Just one of the pauses that they're always rehearsing at the community theater. And before anyone could interrupt him like a bad theater prompter, Alois the Lift says:

"I'm in shock. I'm running so fast to the emergency brake that it nearly does me in. Even though I could tell right away it's no use. But I'm running and I'm slipping on the fresh fallen snow. Underneath it's a plate of ice—don't budge all winter long. That's where the load line snakes around, and up you go, easy, since they're always polishing it with those sharp edges of theirs, all year long, pure formica. Now, I know this—I know every one of the ice sheets around the lift, and I haven't gone down in years. Ha! They're always falling all over the place there, the Dutch girls, because you don't see the crust under the dust. But I do, of course, I know it. But now, I'm so scared that I've forgot. Could've turned out not too pretty, but I just barely catch hold of the emergency brake—and caught myself, too, right on the red emergency brake. That's when it stopped, the lift," Alois the Lift says.

"And I was still standing, too. I walk back to the chair

where the body is, a little shaky in the knees from the shock—nearly took me down. But before I could get to knocking the snow off the corpse, the phone in the cabin starts ringing. Now I don't know: should I knock the snow off the corpse or should I go in and get the phone. But the phone don't stop, and because it's too late anyway, I hurry up and go in."

Maybe the lift operator was exaggerating a little with the pauses, because he raised his beer at this point and took an abnormally long sip.

"Meanwhile, Wörgötter's made it to my lift terminal up top. An old fox, too, that one," Alois the Lift says, smiling.

"But now he's yelling, all excited and beside himself, saying that a body's just come in on the chairlift up there. And right at that moment, when it's at the very tiptop, that's when the lift comes to a halt."

CHAPTER 2

As far as America goes, Zell's a tiny speck. But so far as Pinzgau's concerned: forty hotels, nine schools, thirty mountains over 3,000 meters high, fifty-eight ski lifts, one lake, one detective.

The detective doesn't actually belong to Zell, though. He was only there, of course, on account of the lift scandal. The two Americans froze to death on the chairlift in Zell at the end of December. And here it is, beginning of September, and the detective's still here. He was slowly starting to get the feeling that he wouldn't be getting out of here any time soon.

Like it creeps up on you, that kind of feeling. Or like when you get lost in a labyrinth or you get married and have kids. This is that detective, Brenner's his name. Woke up in a panic a few nights already. Because he dreamed he was prohibited from leaving Zell until he'd solved the hopeless case of the two Americans.

But then he did solve it, even though it'd seemed hopeless to everybody. Now, it was a good three-quarters of a year after the fact, you've got to keep that in mind. Last December, the corpses, and now the next winter season's already at the door. The police gave up before the month of January was out.

Brenner was still on the police force back then. They'd popped up from the city end of December, made a mess out of everything, and by the end of January they'd split again. Nothing and hopeless. Only the *Pinzgauer Post* stayed on it a little while longer. Till mid-February maybe. But, then, done and forgotten.

And beginning of March, all the sudden Brenner turns back up again. But not as police, no, as a detective. Thanks to the insurance company. The deceased were the American in-laws of Vergolder Antretter. About them, you should know, they were stinking rich. Both in their eighties and just filthy rich. Vergolder himself's stinking rich—far and away the richest man in Zell, way above Eder, way above the mayor, leagues above Fürstauer. But, next to his in-laws, a penniless bum.

Needless to say, the Zellers were surprised. First he takes off as police—Brenner, I mean—and then turns back up three weeks later a private detective. Then it comes to light that it's an insurance story, on the Americans' end of things, because for them what it was about was a whole lot of money. Yeah, what do you know. The insurance company doesn't send over their own detective from America, though, because A of all, language problems, and B of all, just easier not to. And cheaper and more efficient and—anyway, they hire a local detective agency. So, they contracted with a detective agency in Vienna. Meierling Detective Agency, it was called.

Now, coincidentally, it turns out that police officer Simon Brenner, Detective Inspector, or whatever his rank was, has quit the police. Now, you should know, he'd been on the force nineteen years. Because he was twenty-five when he started and now he's forty-four. But he never really got anywhere with the police. That wasn't the real reason why he quit, though, because he'd never been especially ambitious. More the quiet type. A nice guy, actually, I've got to admit.

Now, about three years ago, he gets a new boss—Nemec, who turned up here in Zell back in January, too. And him I wouldn't necessarily have wanted for a boss, either. Me, personally, I don't have anything against Wieners—you know, the Viennese—they've got nice ones down there, too, and there are so-and-so's everywhere you go. But he was just such a typical Wiener. Anyway, the two of them just didn't get along at all. Nemec was young and ambitious, and his department just had to be the absolute best. And Brenner, what can I say. Not that he was a bad police officer, certainly not. But, more quieter, low-key, and, well, right off the bat, Nemec just wasn't having it.

He started in on the comments Day One—this was three years ago now—and here in Zell where the whole month of January—well, nothing was going anywhere, so Nemec tries to pin the blame on Brenner. Then, Brenner thinks it over and throws in the towel, by which I mean, his job.

Nowadays when you're forty-four and have spent nineteen of those years on the force, then, a thing like this, you think it over, and I've really got to say, hats off, because, at that moment, he had no prospects of anything else.

Then, Meierling calls him a few days later, you know, the boss of the Meierling Detective Agency. Obviously, Brenner was the ideal candidate because he knew the case. On the other hand, wasn't the highest priority anyway now, let's say, Brenner absolutely having to solve the case. Because it was primarily an insurance matter.

As far as I know, it was more of a formality, you know, that somebody be present until the insurance matters were settled. And that can take years. So that the insurance company can later say, look, we did everything, nobody can blame us for anything, we even sent our own man after the police had long since gave up on the case.

That he'd actually solve the case, well, at that point in time, nobody could've knew that at all.

And today, I really do have to say, hats off to Brenner, because somebody else might not have managed it so easy. A somebody like Nemec might be quicker upstairs, and, on a different case, maybe he's the better bet. But, be it as it may, it was here. The corpses in the lift, foreigners. No witness, no clues, no motive, no nothing! So, once again, Brenner was the right one.

If you'd seen him looking the way he did in Zell, you wouldn't have guessed that he was a private detective. Even though he was no undercover detective. Anybody who wanted to know, they got told—he was there on account of the lift scandal. How should I put it, though: he didn't look like a detective.

The strange thing is that he actually looked exactly like how you might picture a police officer or detective looking. That kind of fireplug type where the shoulders are practically broader than the legs are long. Not big but not small, and a real blockhead with two vertical ruts in his cheeks. And a red, scarred nose like a soccer player—what's his name, quick, the one with the two brothers.

But, I don't think you would've taken him for a detective or a police officer. His aqua-blue eyes surely played a part in that. They're always nervously roaming around, and in retrospect, it's easy to say that it's on account of him always observing everything so closely.

But if you saw him like that, you probably would've just got the impression that he was worried. You'd occasionally see him here and there, on Fussballplatz or at the Feinschmeck Café, or at the Hirschenwirt. Or he'd just be milling around on Kirchplatz or taking a walk down to the lake. And because his face was so red, you could see from a ways away how those blue eyes of his were nervously roaming around. Maybe that's why he wasn't exactly the type to command respect. As a human being, sure, but not, let's say, the way Nemec did.

And that must've been it, too, why Nemec didn't like him—there was just something about him that gave you the sense he didn't belong there. Nemec made fun of it in public:

"Don't go looking like that with those Czech eyes of yours, Brenner!"

Just a few days after Nemec took over the department, that happened. And to make matters worse, in front of

Brenner's co-workers, Tunzinger and Schmeller, who got shot six months later during the bank robbery at the, the, the—now where was that again. Brenner wasn't even aware that he somehow looked strange while he was doing it, and he had no clue what Nemec meant by Czech eyes.

At first he suspected that Nemec possibly had some complex, on account of him having a Czech name. Maybe that's why he made jokes about Czech eyes. Because Brenner had done a whole slew of training sessions in psychology on the force, especially his first years there.

About that, you should know, Nemec was from Vienna, whereas Brenner—Brenner was from Puntigam, you know, where the beer's from, Puntigamer, in Steiermark, by Graz. Now, it wasn't until a year or two later that Brenner found out that the Viennese have all got this idea—or maybe it's just a bunch of talk—that all Czechs have aqua-blue eyes.

But what am I doing talking about Czechs for. After all, the dead bodies were American. They owned a factory in Detroit. And their son-in-law, Vergolder Antretter, well, he owned the chairlift that they were found dead on. The police figured that out Day One, of course. Just never figured out much more than that, though. And now here comes Brenner three-quarters of a year later and figures out who did it!

Now, you should know the kind of person you're dealing with. How should I put it—not easy to describe. For instance, it bothered him when somebody he was on a first-name basis with called him by his last name. But that's how it is on the force: people call each other by their last names.

"What're you doing looking like that with those Czech eyes of yours, Brenner!"

Needless to say, he had to put up with that from his co-workers pretty often, because needless to say, Schmeller and Tunzinger didn't keep it to themselves. And when six months later they shot Schmeller, well, it didn't do him any good, because his other co-workers had caught on in the meanwhile and kept on saying it, too.

But that wasn't what was giving him a headache. Not the thing about the Czech eyes and not the thing with the name. Only one thing that could give Brenner a royal headache like this, and that was his own head.

About his head, you should know, on the day he quit the force, he also, out of some kind of, I don't know, quit smoking. And ever since that day, at least twice a month he gets a migraine that leaves him barely able to see out of those Czech eyes of his.

Of course, he couldn't be sure: was it from quitting smoking—basically withdrawal, because he smoked forty a day. Or did it have to do with the career change, why he was getting headaches more often than he used to get, from the worrying. Or, third possibility, it was just the weather in Zell that didn't agree with him, especially now, this heat in September, just unnatural.

Anyway. His head was the reason why Brenner was showing up now at the Zell pharmacy and demanding a pack of Migradon from Ewalt the pharmacist.

"For whom are these tablets intended, Herr Brenner?"

"For me."

17

"Have you seen a doctor about this condition?"

Brenner now, headache already so bad that he didn't know where to look—well, the young pharmacist struck him as being a little long-winded.

"Yeah," he murmured, and was already out the door before the pharmacist could make herself important.

You should know, "Czech eyes"—not what the women were thinking, no, "child's eyes." And add to that, two ruts a centimeter deep in his cheeks, and in a skull with four blunt edges, no less. Needless to say, most of them liked that.

He was in a hurry now to get to his hotel room, though. First, take the pills, then, type up the report for the week. Because every week he had to submit a report to the Meierling Detective Agency. And this week he hadn't done it yet. And he had the feeling he wasn't going to get rid of this headache, pills or no pills. It was three o'clock now, the post office closes at five-thirty, and Brenner wanted to get his report in today's mail. So he had to hurry, only two hours left for the whole report.

Needless to say, to find a familiar face waiting there in the dingy lobby of the Hirschenwirt, well, he was none too happy. Nor was he happy to hear a familiar voice addressing him at the same time. Both belonged to a young man with a tie green as poison on which the word "okay" was printed over and over in all different sizes.

"A little respect, Herr Inspector!" the young man says and makes an idiotic salute.

"Mandl," Brenner grumbles. He noticed right away how it'd already began its descent, his dread of the lacquered local reporter with the aristocratic manners.

"There's no kaiser anymore, Mandl."

"There's a Lift Kaiser, a Village Kaiser, a Real Estate Kaiser!" Mandl countered so fast that his head gave a little jerk, causing a strand of hair to come loose. Because it'd been glued down with gel, and now it was standing straight up and quivering, just unnatural.

Back when he was still on the force, Brenner used to tease him sometimes and instead of Mandl he'd call him "Myrtle." But he hadn't had anything to do with the reporter from the *Pinzgauer Post* for some time now. And today, no desire at all, because A of all, headache, and B of all, a report to finally get sent off.

Even though the report wasn't all that urgent. Quite the opposite. Meierling—you know, the boss of the detective agency—his name wasn't actually Meierling but Brugger—had warned Brenner several times that he shouldn't write such pitifully long reports. And last week he even gave orders that if Brenner couldn't keep it brief, he should kindly include a ten-line summary as an abstract.

"Nobody reads what you write!" he said, just had to go rubbing Brenner's nose in it. Now, you should know Brenner's motto. Because, his motto, write everything down, important or unimportant. And in retrospect, you've got to admit, he was right.

But now of all times, just when he felt like things were gradually falling into place, Mandl gets in his way.

But, to be perfectly honest, that was only half the truth, why Detective Brenner was in such a lousy mood just then. Listen up, it happened like this. Mandl asks:

"You on duty, Herr Inspector?" Even though it'd been

over half a year since Brenner had been on the force. And Mandl knew that for a fact.

Brenner, though, he doesn't let anything show, no, he says, "I'm always on duty, Mandl."

"And when's quittin' time?"

"As soon as I've caught him."

"So, it's a him—male perp, lone operator."

Mandl actually talked this way. I've got to be honest, he wasn't as bad as everyone made him out to be. He was still young and wanting to make something of himself at the newspaper. But Brenner could only shake his head at this degree of useless enthusiasm.

"You've got a lot to learn, Mandl."

Mandl had got him this far, though. He motioned to the waitress for two glasses of white. The Hirschenwirt is one of these old inns with an enormous bar in the lobby, and the two men just happened to be standing in front of it. The waitress set their wineglasses down, and Mandl pulled a violet fifty out of his poison-green shirt pocket. It was enough to make Brenner sick.

"You trying to lose your very last reader, too?" the detective asks now.

"What, we've got a reader?" Mandl asks, and grins like for the dentist commercials, because ever since his report about the underground bordello in the Brucker Bundesstrasse, he'd had two brand-new crowns put in.

"With an old story like this, you won't be coaxing anybody away from the fireside anyhow."

"Don't got a dog, eh? Write an old story, roll up the

newspaper, and throw it. Dog fetches newspaper. Leaves his spot by the fire. Police seize opportunity. Park themselves by the fire. Eh?"

"What're you getting at? And why're you always calling me police?"

"At what, Inspector? It's: *At what are you getting?* Because: *From where'd you get your grammar?*"

How should I put it. Mandl wasn't putting nothin' in nobody's way. He just felt like he had to knock the whole world down, sheer self-importance. Brenner only said:

"You know what I think? I think you did it. Perverse like you are."

"So, a lone operator, good-looking, perverse? That reminds me of something—where exactly is the American?"

"In America."

But this was another American that the two of them were talking about. Not the old millionairess from the lift. And this is what I've been trying to say this whole time. Why Brenner was in such a foul mood.

You should know, an agent from the American insurance company was in Zell for a few weeks. And from the start, she had something to do with Brenner because he was practically employed by the insurance company, too. That was one blond young American, the likes of which we only know from the movies over here. Or if you can imagine a Barbie doll. Betty was her name. And she was in Zell practically the whole summer.

Naturally there was gossip. Not just Mandl was after her, but more or less every character in Zell, and when it comes to something like this, there are always a couple old slack-jaws, of course. But that wasn't the gossip. Because none of the Zellers had any success with the American. So other rumors got invented. That she was actually an American undercover agent. Sent extra by the FBI. Some said CIA, too, and a few even Scotland Yard, but then, Fürstauer over at the deli, he knew that that's only in Scotland.

Betty was just from the insurance company, though. She was doing some type of local visit to the scene of the crime, and from Brenner she got everything she could ever want to know about the case. He couldn't offer her much, though. I mean, in so far as the case goes, he couldn't offer her very much.

And so far as that goes, I'll only say this much. She also had a room at the Hirschenwirt. And she'd been, ever since she was *ein kleines Mädchen*, a little girl over in America, she'd been in love with Robert Redford. Now, Brenner looks nothing like Robert Redford, but something about him must've reminded her of Robert Redford.

That was in August. And now the first week of September's almost over, and Mandl's just standing there in the Hirschenwirt lobby and asking:

"Where exactly is the American?"

What I'm getting at with this. I think it's actually because of that. Why the moment for small talk was passing Brenner by. And when he noticed how disappointed and pale Mandl suddenly got, Brenner pounced again and said:

"The American? The American's in America."

It was only then that he noticed how it was doing him

more harm than it was the local reporter. But he didn't let anything show. Simply turned around and left Mandl standing there with their two wineglasses. Then he went upstairs and finally tried to write his report. Sending it off, though, that he could always do tomorrow.

CHAPTER 3

Nowadays when a person goes around trying to force something at all costs, there's no way it's going to work. Maybe that was the reason why Brenner still hadn't wrote a single word of his report for the Meierling Detective Agency. Even though it'd been a solid hour since he'd left Mandl standing back there.

It was the sixth of September, but still warm enough that he could sit in his room in his bare chest. The rooms on the shady side of the inn, well, another story altogether this time of year. Brenner's room was sunnyside, though, so needless to say, it heats up something awful during the day, whew, let me tell you.

For over an hour he'd been sitting at that small table in his room, when all of the sudden he realized—he still hadn't written a line. Because in his thoughts, he was somewhere else completely. That was his old malady, that he couldn't concentrate. Outwardly, Brenner gave the impression of being horribly calm. There's that movie where the monk says—you know, an Indian, a Buddhist—he says: If I go, then I go, and if I stay, then I stay. And that's the kind of impression a person gets of Brenner if you see him going or staying—or as far as I'm concerned, sitting—somewhere. All a facade.

And you'd have to know him pretty well in order to know how anxious he was all the time. And focusing on the essentials, let's say, that wasn't his strong suit at all. Nemec, he recognized this Day One and just had to rub Brenner's nose right in it:

"Concentrate instead of ruminate, Brenner!"

Because that was Nemec's answer when Brenner asked him if he could take a professional development course. Maybe it's not that wise, either, when you've got a new boss, to ask for professional development on the guy's very first day, since it's going to mean at least two days out of the office. Brenner must've been thinking of that just now when he realized he hadn't wrote a single word, even though he'd been staring at his table for an hour already.

Such a small filigree table, I mean, all you had to do was look at it, and it'd wobble. And you couldn't imagine anyone using it for anything but looking at. Brenner, though. To him, this sort of thing didn't matter. He had been typing up his reports here, week in, week out, for six months.

His grandfather back in Puntigam had been a carpenter. A thing like this he never would've called a table. Brenner still had two cabinets that his grandfather built. Nice, slim walnut units that'd been there in his parents' apartment since before he came into this world.

And ever since his parents died, Brenner had them in his apartment. Because he didn't have any siblings, and they fit in good with his government-subsidized apartment. Well, civil service apartment, since only civil servants live there—cheap rent, let me tell you. And now, of course,

Brenner was afraid he'd have to move out since he quit the police.

And then something happened that surprised him. Because up till now he still hadn't heard anything—no written notice, nothing. And instead of finally writing his report, he thinks now: Probably has to do with his old school chum Schwaighofer. Basically, it went something like this:

When Brenner put in a request for an apartment as in-demand as this one was five years ago, he was in for a surprise. At first he didn't recognize him, because, bald and twenty years since he'd seen him, but his old classmate Schwaighofer recognized him right away. He was the office manager there and responsible for the allocation of the apartments. At first it was uncomfortable for Brenner, awkward, you know, because what do you talk about with a person when the last time you saw him was twenty years ago. And, even back then, they didn't really talk all that much. Brenner had always been a bit of a closed book, you can't forget. I don't want to say stubborn, but shut off all the time. And Schwaighofer, too, never anything remarkable, that guy.

It didn't stay uncomfortable for long, though, because, as a bachelor, he'd be put on a wait-list—yes, they've got wait-lists for these—years!—don't even ask. Then, three months later, he's moving in, and goes without saying, his classmate Schwaighofer had made the arrangements. That's the way we do it over here. The same everywhere.

And now, because he hadn't heard anything in six months from the Civil Service Housing Authority, i.e. Schwaighofer, Brenner was slowly starting to get his hopes up. That possibly his classmate Schwaighofer was behind it, and there'd been some oversight—on purpose, I mean, computer or whatnot—about Brenner having to move out.

That's neither here nor there. But for Brenner, things weren't exactly going any different. He's sitting in his hot room and he's supposed to be thinking about work, but instead he's thinking about his apartment. And hear me out, what I'm about to tell you now. Coincidence it was not, because—coincidence, well, there's no such thing, it's been proved.

Instead of the report now, Brenner must've been thinking about that one time he took his co-worker Anni Bichler back to his apartment. Anni, that was one of the two secretaries in his department, but the prettier one. This was a good five years ago that he took Anni home with him, because he'd just moved into his civil service apartment a few weeks before that. The next morning over breakfast, Anni says:

"Frankly—"

Now, you should know, if there's one thing Brenner can't stand. When someone begins a sentence with "frankly." He'd become convinced somehow that sentences like that—that start off like that, with "frankly," I mean—that they never amount to anything good.

He was in for a surprise now, though, because Anni Bichler said something completely different. Because he would've expected his colleague, Ms. Bichler, to maybe complain that he'd taken advantage of her in her condition, i.e. plastered.

The fact of the matter was that he himself couldn't remember all the details from the night before. Only this much is certain: that the woman who was spreading apricot jam on her toast there at breakfast was his colleague from the office, Secretary Bichler. And that he'd agreed to switch over to a first-name basis with her over a drink yesterday at the birthday party of another colleague of theirs, Schmeller, who was then shot to death two and a half years later during the bank robbery.

But he didn't know much more than that—above all if he'd actually slept with Anni. But she probably did know, and that's probably why she was opening her mouth now to complain about something that Brenner, despite his best efforts, possibly didn't even remember.

"Frankly, your apartment doesn't have any atmosphere."

Brenner was momentarily relieved. But it was only momentarily a relief. Because it struck him later that when a woman starts fannying around with your furnishings, this might mean something. Okay, in good German: Serious Intentions. But, not to worry, because Anni, just super, at the office she acted like nothing had happened.

And maybe nothing actually did happen, or possibly something did happen but neither one of them remembered, but—whatever, it's no concern of mine, because it's got nothing to do with who Ted Parson and his wife, her name was Suzanne, who put these old people on the chairlift.

But then, two weeks after the story with Bichler, okay, Anni, was at the police ball. And Brenner brings the Precinct Music Director's daughter back to his new civil service apartment. And that's when it slowly, bizarrely began to dawn on—well, how should I put it: realization. Because the Precinct Music Director's daughter hadn't even took off her shoes yet before she was saying:

"I don't know, somehow your apartment doesn't have any atmosphere."

The very next weekend he was having those two walnut cabinets moved into his apartment. And not just had them moved, but he had cabinets that don't come apart moved into the third floor of a civil service apartment building. It was by the skin of their teeth that they even got them up there, but believe it or not: no use.

Because the next weekend, or the weekend after that, he gets paid another visit. Brenner wasn't exactly choosy in that sense of the word, and this was one hell of—but please, I could care less. Anyway, short and sweet, she said:

"Your apartment somehow doesn't have any atmosphere at all."

Now, why am I telling you all of this. Brenner's sitting in his hotel room at the Hirschenwirt and waiting for his migraine pills to finally kick in. And instead of writing his report, he's staring at the veneered table and thinking of the walnut cabinets from his grandfather. Those nervous blue eyes of his weren't roaming nervously around now at all. But not because they were fixated on the table, because they weren't, really. What they were really doing is looking *through* the table. The table and the whole hotel-room atmosphere didn't bother Brenner one bit.

There was just one thing that did bother him. That he

couldn't concentrate. And that was what Nemec was always getting on him about, too. And Brenner didn't know any better than to secretly admit now that Nemec was right.

Only one thing I can say about that. It was no coincidence. Nobody would've been able to concentrate on this case. Because there wasn't anything there for you to set your sights on. What are you supposed to concentrate on when there's nothing there. And another thing that's no coincidence. That Brenner of all people, who wasn't exactly the focused type, either, that, in the end, he of all people was the right one to have on a case like this.

Because it's like black ice, or the way I see it, deep snow, or compare it to something else if you want. You'll need a different gait to go forward better than you would on, say, asphalt. And here's a person who's way too, circumspect, let's say, and slow, even on asphalt, but who's possibly got an advantage in the end.

And a person who cuts a good figure eight on the asphalt like Nemec, let's say, who marches blindly forward—a real comedy—somebody who, goes without saying, falls flat on his face right from the get-go—what a farce.

The police investigation back in January led to absolute squat. At first, beginning of January, this meant that there were two leads that they had to keep secret about. And by the end of January, they'd cleared out again, and there wasn't any more talk of leads.

"No stone shall go unturned," was Nemec's motto at the beginning. Or that's how it appeared in the PP anyway. In the *Pinzgauer Post*. And on top of that, get this, Nemec made it seem like he'd be smoking the culprit out of his hole within a matter of hours. Or better put:

"Smoke the culprit out of his, or her—or their—hole," because Nemec was always jumping in and correcting everybody like that if they talked about anybody. A person need only say "he," and she could be sure that Nemec would interrupt her:

"He or she or they."

"Or it!" Brenner would correct Nemec again. And this in front of his coworker, Tunzinger! Because Schmeller, well, a year and a half before, during that bank robbery at the, uh, the—well, he got shot there.

Now, I don't mean to say that Nemec had an especially meaty face. Although he is thin, skin and bones, really. But more like peptic-ulcer thin. No, not that either—more like a student. It was actually a real babyface that he had. Over forty, that I know, but if you saw him on the street, you might take him for thirty, for just a student with wire-rimmed glasses.

And maybe it's on account of his kiddish face that a person's apt to notice. Because when he was fed up, a blue vein thick as your finger would, believe it or not, pop up out of his forehead. And the harder he tried not to let his anger show, the thicker the blue vein on his forehead would swell up. You'd have thought that all the anger he was trying to suppress just got pumped straight into his forehead vein.

But, apart from the blue vein, he showed no reaction to the scene that Brenner made back there, I mean, him saying "it." This was end of January already. And people already knew about it, the whole bungled mess.

Two leads starting out, but now, no leads at all anymore. And for those two leads, the police only got laughed at by the Zellers anyway.

But I have to be honest, what else were they supposed to do. Vergolder was the victims' only blood relative, so they started with him. A motive, well—he had one. Because he'd stand to inherit a few million—and, no, not what you're thinking, Austrian schillings. Because, America, and over there the dollar is legal tender. But since he himself owned half of Zell and since he's not that stupid to have—I mean, his own in-laws on his own ski lift in Zell—what can I say, end of January, the police realized it, too.

Maybe, well, it wouldn't surprise me. Maybe it just irritated Nemec that Vergolder was one of the bigwigs in town. And so they were practically asking the mayor or the priest for an alibi.

At the time, I think Nemec was already picturing himself in the newspapers, heroic exposé or something, and a photo of him alongside, Uncompromising and Incorruptible. But they couldn't prove anything on Vergolder, and needless to say, a disgrace of the first order for Nemec. End of January, suddenly there was no more talk of Vergolder.

And the "Heidnische Kirche," I don't dare speak of that, because that was the second lead, but even less than nothing came of that. But Brenner must've been thinking about the "Heidnische Kirche" now, too, but for a different reason. Because he put his shirt back on and went out onto the balcony off his hotel room at the Hirschenwirt.

Down at the lake it was high season just a week ago,

and now, just a few lone swimmers. It was the beginning of September, way too warm for this time of year, like the weatherman was always claiming. But school had started in spite of it. The vacationers disappeared overnight, only a few retirees were still here.

And Brenner, of course. He was still here, too. And this feeling he's got—that's why it's so dangerous when a detective relies on his feelings. Because this feeling he had just an hour ago that gave him a sense of hope, now, as he was standing there on his balcony and looking out over the lake, he felt completely hopeless all of the sudden.

One thing's gotta be said, a magnificent sight. And the mountains so close, you couldn't believe there was a lake in between. He could've looked all the way to the reservoir now, no problem. But a wooded outcropping obstructed his view of the area, which, in the hiking maps from the old days, was called "Heidnische Kirche."

"Heidnische Kirche" is the way the threat letters are signed that turn up in the op-ed section of the *Pinzgauer Post*. And the claims in these letters, I mean, listen to this, either a madman or a prankster wrote them: The Zell community ought to—just imagine, all the skiing. Shut down. The whole industry. Eradicated! And if that doesn't happen, then the Mooser Dam, blown to pieces. That's exactly how it was written in the letters. Signed: Heidnische Kirche.

Now, you can't forget that here above Zell is—well, really in Glocknermassiv, but practically right over the heads of the Zellers—one of the biggest dams in all of Europe. People don't realize this at all when they're passing through

Zell. That it's over them—practically Damocles, if it breaks, a dam like that. Because the Mooser Dam, that's one of the three dam walls. And it's located practically right in the middle of this area that's called "Heidnische Kirche." Where the name comes from, nobody knows.

And then there's the Drossen Dam and the Limberg Dam, too, the other two dam walls. It's impossible, of course, for a dam to actually break. But let's say it's not. When it breaks, don't even bother worrying about there being any survivors from Zell.

On the other hand. The dam's been up there for almost fifty years because the reservoir was opened right after the war. "Symbol of the Republic," it said in the newspaper, that was 1951 when they opened it. Nowadays, of course, you couldn't build a reservoir high up in the mountains in just six years. Or maybe you could today, but back then, you couldn't. The politicians, of course, didn't lose any sleep over it, about the whole—but I don't want to get started in on the Nazi years now.

By the twenty-five year anniversary, critical reporting was all the rage, more or less. And a few years ago, that would be 1991, that was the forty-year anniversary. They even invited a few of the Ukrainian POWs because hundreds of them had died up there on the construction site during the War. It was the Americans, then, who finished building the reservoir.

After the war, everybody was glad about the electricity and about the upswing, and the politicians called the reservoir the "Symbol of the Republic." So maybe it was on account of the "Heidnische Kirche" that Nemec guessed political terrorism or something like that, but the people down here aren't real political.

The police only came up with the idea because of the ski tourism, I mean, on account of the demand that it be shut down. Because the dead bodies. In the ski lift of all places. Because that's deliberate. Practically a final warning. But there was no letter accompanying it, no phone calls, either, and so what kind of a warning's that, really.

And then it got pointed out that this kind of threat is as old as the reservoir itself. Somehow the reservoir just stirs people's imaginations. Maybe some anxiety, unconscious, I don't know. The mayor of Zell had a whole collection of these letters. But the cops were here three weeks already before they found out about them. Because you've got to see to it that something like this doesn't make its way into the public. Imagine if the tourists stayed away, possibly on account of some nonsense like this.

And the mayor always said: "Blow up a wall ten meters thick? It would be easier to blow away the mountains all around it."

But in the council meeting minutes, well, sentences like these never made their way in. Because someone saw to it that it didn't become official, let's say, more like dead silent. And for the best. Because the reservoir's still up there.

Brenner was thinking that, too, now, as he looked out at it from his balcony. The reservoir's still up there, and nothing else has changed, either. Because if he was going to be honest, then he, too, a full half a year later now, still didn't have a lead. And Brenner was in exactly the kind of mood where a person's bound to get honest with himself.

The sun was slowly going down, and the lake was gleaming. Now there's nature putting on a show, enough to make you say: unreal, nothing like it.

And it occurred to him that he was being about as thick as the Precinct Music Director's daughter when, silently, he says to himself now:

"Frankly, it wasn't the Heidnische Kirche, and it wasn't Vergolder Antretter, either, and it wasn't anybody else, either. But it must've been somebody."

CHAPTER 4

No, no, now look here. Zell's not so small that everybody knows everybody else. But everybody does know Goggenberger, the taxi driver, Johnny. He's an original, alright—you can say that again. Because he's 120 kilos and got a pink Chevrolet that he's been driving around Zell for twenty years. He's never done anything else, because, Johnny's not quite as old as he looks. But where he got the Chevrolet from, that's what I'd be interested to know.

Now, on the seventh of September, Brenner had Johnny drive him to Kaprun. It was more, let's say, not because Brenner absolutely had to go to Kaprun. But because taxi drivers, often times they hear a lot. And if he has Johnny take him somewhere, then maybe I'll learn something, Brenner thought, but then it backfired on him.

Because, Johnny, he don't say moo or baa. And even if you drove all the way up to Sweden with him. Because once a Swede broke his foot skiing, and he had Johnny chauffeur him all the way home to Sweden. And I have to say, enjoyable, that cannot have been, because Johnny smokes Virginias, and the stench in that Chevrolet of his—you can barely put up with it from Zell to Schüttdorf. And needless to say, he didn't do much in the way of talking with the Swede, either, because the Swede didn't know any German, and Johnny, well, I have yet to hear him say anything in Swedish.

"I'll be damned!" Johnny's saying now, as the weatherman reports on the radio that it's going to be even hotter today than yesterday.

Otherwise, Brenner didn't get anything out of him. When he's drunk, Johnny talks nonstop, so when he's quiet, it's nonstop too. He's rarely drunk, though, because, as a cabbie, he can't afford it, of course, not one bit.

But there was something else bothering Brenner even more. Not the Virginia stench, though, because today his headache was completely gone, and so it wasn't anything like that bothering him. He himself used to smoke up till about seven months ago. No, it was the fact that Johnny took the two-lane county road where every normal person drives 100 because, highway, you know—and you could even drive a nice leisurely 150, if they allowed it. And Johnny's taking it at a steady 50!

Because Johnny—the Zellers know this, of course, but the outsiders get annoyed about it time and again—he's never driven faster than fifty. But it was bothering Brenner, and that's why he says, middle of the ride:

"I'll get out here."

"Here?"

"Yeah."

"I'll be damned."

Johnny was surprised because there wasn't anything around where Brenner got out. All of two kilometers outside

Zell. But, go a couple hundred meters up toward Kaprun, there's this barn that you probably know, the one that's got those old ads hanging up. "The good old brandy," it says. You can barely read it anymore. But remove it, of course, nobody does that either, because the ad's painted right onto the wall.

Brenner hadn't seen this ad-painting before, though. He was still watching the pink Chevrolet as it made a big show of turning around and peeling back off toward Zell again, practically at a walk. His miscalculation about Johnny wasn't bothering him at all anymore. He could tell as soon as he woke up that morning that it was going to be another beautiful, sunny fall day. And then, right away he realized that he wasn't any happier about having to write that report today, either. So, the ride with the cabbie was also a bit of an excuse. Because Brenner just wanted to get out a little, instead of just sitting in his hotel room and writing his report. He's walking across the mowed field now and around to the barn, and he's just seen the ad. "The good old brandy," it says, but completely weathered, and Brenner's wondering how many years or decades it's been here.

One thing was certain, though. That the ad was at least twenty-five years old. For that you don't need a laboratory or nothing, because the ad was facing the wrong direction. Not facing out to the street, but away from the street.

Because twenty-five years ago the highway got put in here, I mean, the one that Johnny still only drives fifty on. But the ad's on the other side of the barn, the side that, from the street, you can't see at all. Because that's where the old road went by, and today it's all broken up and got grass growing out of it.

Only, right here where the barn is, the road's still intact. Okay, what am I saying—she's got even better asphalt than the new highway, and the new one's already been asphalted over three times in the meantime. But those 200 meters of old road, that was the Zellers' summer curling strip, which Brenner also didn't know about until now.

He watched the curling for a little while—it was about twelve-thirty now, not a cloud in the sky, I mean, beautiful days like this, there just aren't that many of them in Zell. And Brenner just couldn't imagine anymore who would kill somebody here, because, nothing's more peaceful than summer Alpine curling.

Aside from Brenner, there was only one other spectator standing on the side of the road, but up at the other end, and Brenner couldn't really recognize him from where he was. The other players were up at the other end now, too, and were sending their stocks sliding one after another. I mean, you've got to picture it like how they sometimes show it on TV, in France, with the silver pucks. And shuffleboard's more of a sport for retirees anyway, but you don't do Alpine curling with shuffle pucks, no, with ice stocks. And so that the stocks will glide over an asphalt court in the summer, you screw these little white plastic tacks into their undersides.

But Brenner was just thinking that there's nothing more peaceful than this little crew of retirees, when, all of the sudden, things got out of hand. He didn't understand what the fight was about at first.

Now, pay attention. With curling, it's about the money, not much, but because it wouldn't be any fun otherwise. There are always two teams, okay. And each shooter trades off with one from the other team. So, how much money they're playing for—even though they're playing on teams—basically comes down to two players. Let's say, a pair's playing for ten schillings, okay. That doesn't need to be exact—you only ever need to find a pair that can take turns back and forth. And if your team wins, then you get the money, and otherwise you pay.

But not what you're thinking, that they were fighting on account of the money. That doesn't happen, because, I mean—done is done. It was more on account of, let's say, because there are better shooters and worser ones, and the retirees are just like little kids when it comes to this. Everybody believes he's one of the better ones. Which wouldn't settle a thing if everybody believed what they wanted to. But, see, there's this problem, the "Haggl," and believe it or not, a fight every time.

Every team's got a leader, though, like soccer's got a captain. Theirs was a "Moar"—don't ask me where it comes from, that's just its name—and he gets to shoot twice. Everybody else is only allowed to shoot once, but after everybody's gone, the team's still got one last chance, because that's when the Moar goes up one more time. Now, who's the Moar. That's very highly regulated, because it's always the best shooter from the previous game—automatically the Moar. There's never a fight over that, but with the Haggl, there's gladly a fight.

Now, what's a Haggl? Nowadays when you've got a few retirees, and a few others who've maybe just got the time on their hands, playing curling on an afternoon, then it's not like at a tournament—I mean, officially regulated, and on each side, such-and-such number of players. It can turn out, just happenstance, not to be an even number, and so, one team's got one man more than the other, let's say, eight on the one side, nine on the other. So, on the one team where there's less, somebody's the Haggl. He's allowed to shoot twice, then, just like the Moar.

And so, of course, there's always a fight, because nothing on the books about who the Haggl is—the best, obviously. It's better for the whole team when a good player gets to shoot twice. But what's the point of that when everybody believes he's the best.

"You, the Haggl?" yelled a small, gaunt man that Brenner didn't know. He had dirty rubber boots on and an old felt hat on his head. That was Gschwentner the farmer. And the one who he meant, that was Andi the Fox, he was just eighteen or nineteen but already completely bald.

"You bet. If you want to win your fiver back."

The others had a good laugh over that one from Andi the Fox, who was getting cocky about defending his post as Haggl. Now, you should know, Gschwentner the farmer only looked like some poor farmer. But he's the biggest farmer for miles around—and stingy, you wouldn't believe. And it was his stinginess that Andi meant. That he was playing for a fiver, even though the ante usually starts at ten.

Brenner laughed, too. He was just happy that his

patience had frayed here of all places and that he'd gotten out of Johnny's pink Chevrolet. Of course he had no idea at the time that this would be the place where he'd find what he'd been looking for from Johnny, the cabbie. That here, in the middle of this petty quarreling of all things, he'd discover a lead. Just so you know, he wasn't counting on this at all right now.

Now, pay attention to how it all unfolds. The players are all standing at the top of the court and Brenner's down on the other end, waiting for them to begin their curling. And then, one after another, the players make their way down to the other end, because every one of them, of course, goes down there after his shot. And it's only just now that Brenner recognizes Vergolder Antretter. He was the Moar on the other team, i.e., not Gschwentner and Andi's team but the opposite team, and he'd just taken his first shot and was making his way down to where Brenner's standing now.

Brenner was surprised that Vergolder shot stock with the common folk. Because normally he went with very different people. The German Bundespräsident had a house in the vicinity, or the head of the regional government would come for a visit, and those were Vergolder's people. The mayor didn't exactly go shooting stock, either—at most once a year, or when there was an election.

Then, turns out that Vergolder's first shot was so good— the whole opposing team, one shot, practically annihilated. Because he caught the pigeon with his stock—right, so, that's the goal of curling, the pigeon, that's just this little wooden box—and with so much force that his stock took its target with it and left it lodged right between the stock and the bumper.

Now, the other team was up, one after another giving it a go, but jinxed. The stocks got tossed into the air, either too hard and just went whistling right by, or too soft and just became obstacles blocking the way. So it was impossible for anybody to shoot away Vergolder's stock.

What can I say, all eight of them shot, and Vergolder's stock, still stuck on the pigeon—you'd have thought it was frozen right onto it. Now the Haggl was up, he had a second chance to give it a go. Andi the Fox grabbed his stock, went back up and positioned himself for his second shot. At that moment, though, as he was sizing things up for the longest time and swinging his stock back and forth for the longest time, Vergolder yells out:

"C'mon Andi, full-service, unleaded!"

Now, you can imagine the kind of laughter that got. Because Andi, he's a gas jockey, and then Vergolder goes and breaks his concentration, shouting out:

"C'mon Andi, full-service, unleaded!"

Brenner didn't understand at first why everybody was laughing like that, because he couldn't have knew that Andi was a gas jockey. Because Brenner didn't have a car in Zell— he was more of a walker.

But the other onlooker, who'd at first been standing way up on the other end of the asphalt court, had, by now, come over. But that was no spectator, rather a spectatress. An old woman with thick bifocals. But there was something else about her that was way more conspicuous. On account of her not having any hands.

She was standing next to Brenner, and he asked her if she understood why the people were laughing like that.

"The boy is a gas station attendant," the woman said, and in High German.

At first Brenner was surprised that a German would be out here watching Alpine curling. Because it's more of a local matter. But he quickly got distracted because things were really throwing down now on the asphalt court.

Because, meanwhile, the gas jockey had took his shot, but, way off. And now he'd stormed over, head completely red, and was threatening to give Vergolder the business. And you've just got to picture this: Vergolder, a snow-white, seventy-year-old millionaire, and Andi, who seemed more or less, well, not especially smart. He had his dirty gas-station pants on, he had his bald head, and he was running right at Vergolder now, asking him if perchance he'd like a piece of him.

For the next game, new teams, and they didn't need a Haggl anymore. They were an even number now, because Andi wasn't playing anymore. He sulked over to the kiosk: "Beer," he says to Gruntner Schorsch, who used to work for the train, and now, in his retirement, he runs this kiosk. But today just wasn't Andi's day, because Gruntner just says:

"Hold on a sec."

This was on account of him having two other customers to serve. In front of Andi at the sausage stand were Brenner and the handless old Frau. And Brenner was in shock now, because from a distance, he'd guessed Andi to be forty, if not fifty, and he was just now seeing that he was at most seventeen or eighteen years old.

Andi the Fox had on his red overalls from the gas station like he always did. On the bib Brenner recognized the outline of a Shell seashell that must've once been sewed on there, but now the fabric was just a shade darker in that spot, not as washed-out as it was all around it. Like an old man standing there, Brenner thought, but then it was the exact opposite once Andi started talking.

"Hold on a sec, hold on a sec, so I should just, a second, huh, that's what I should do, huh, hold on?" the Haggl was so giddy talking to the kiosk owner with his high-pitched croak of a voice that you'd have thought his voice hadn't changed yet—practically a eunuch. And at the same time, he was looking at Brenner anxiously, like, Is he maybe on my side, will he laugh at my jokes? But Andi didn't give him any time for all that, because practically in the same breath he was already saying something else again:

"You sure got it figured out, Detective."

Brenner had never tried to somehow make a secret out of it or anything. It's always been an old rift, undercover detective or more of an official—well, dis- and advantages, there's always been people from both camps. Trade rags for cops, trade rags for detectives, whatever else there is, it's been discussed again and again.

It always reminded Brenner of his first two years on the force. Because he was still on the traffic patrol back then. And it was constantly getting discussed, what's better:

secret radar surveillance, or blatant warning: Caution, Radar. Taken together, what scared the speedsters off more.

In his case, though, it'd been clear from the start, I mean, undercover or not undercover. The Zellers already knew him from the police, so, undercover, that wouldn't have worked anyway. And oftentimes, it's no disadvantage at all when people start making themselves important like Andi the Fox was doing right now.

"I said, you sure got it figured out, Detective. Because everybody's a crook. Don't have to go looking for very long down here, crooks, all of 'em. Gschwentner. Vergolder. Millionaire, but never tips a penny. Clean the windshield, sure, tip, no. Check the coolant, yes please, tip, no thanks, have a look at the air pressure, Andi, tip, sorry no, Herr Crook. No time, Herr Millionaire. Gotta work the nightshift, lifting the Ameri-can'ts."

Andi sure liked that, what he'd just come up with in his rage, so much so that he turned around now and yelled over to Vergolder Antretter:

"Lifting the American'ts, Mister Antretter. Want your *regening?*"

But Vergolder didn't react at all. And the others didn't laugh, either, because they didn't dare laugh in front of Vergolder.

"Get it, Detective? *Regening?* In Dutch it means: Do you want your check? Holland's the best country for tips. Vienna's good, too. What's with you, Detective? What, no beer? When are you finally gonna catch the crook?"

Brenner bought a sausage on a bun and then asked Andi,

after he had taken a bite, in other words, with his mouth full:

"Who should I arrest then? Gschwentner or Vergolder?"

"Nah, Detective, you'd better not arrest anybody, how stupid do you really think I am?"

Brenner had this unusual habit. He was one of those people who—okay, when they're eating a sausage on a bun, they only unwrap the paper-wrapper halfway. Because on the end where there's still paper on it, that's where they hold the bun. Frankly, I've never gotten my fingers dirty from a bun, but please!

As he was unwrapping his sausage halfway, he noticed that Gruntner, in his early retirement, had had his name printed on the napkins. Gruntner used to work for the train, as a shunter, and it shaved his left leg off, so now he's retired and still works a little at the kiosk.

He makes a good sausage on a bun, Brenner was thinking when he heard Andi say:

"Should I tell you who put those two Americans in the lift?"

But Brenner just wanted to eat his sausage in peace now and gave Andi no reply. He just looked through Andi, straight through to the curling practically. But Andi wouldn't give it a rest:

"There are only two in question. Either Gschwentner or Vergolder."

"This is the second time you've said that now," Brenner says, without looking away from the curling.

"The preacher don't preach twice," Andi says.

"So be it."

"But I'm no preacher. I'm a gas station attendant. And only a gas station attendant can know what I know."

"What do you know, then?" Brenner asks now, but he's still watching the curling. But that was just what it seemed like. Because out of the corner of his eye, he's observing how the handless Frau drinks her beer.

She simply wedges the beer glass between her forearm-stumps, and that's how she drinks, but not what you're thinking, cautiously, or, as far as I'm concerned, unappetizingly. No, just like you'd have thought, perfectly normal for a person to drink like that. And smoked, too, at the same time. Because she was a smoker, and not just a few. Practically with her wrists. And interesting. This was the first time in months that Brenner was tempted to smoke again, too.

Brenner realized now that this couldn't be the first time that the woman had come here. Without asking any questions, Gruntner Schorsch placed a second empty beer glass on this wooden ledge that went around the kiosk. And on top of the empty beer glass he put an ashtray, and so the handless Frau was able to set her cigarette down right from her mouth without any problem. Needless to say, couldn't have been any easier.

It struck Brenner as being somewhat strange now, the one only had one leg, the other no hands, but that's the way it was.

"I know there are only two people in all of Zell that come

into question with a crime like this," Andi just wouldn't let up and was wagging his finger in front of Brenner's face now like a know-it-all.

"Vergolder and Gschwentner," Brenner answered.

"That's exactly right," Andi the Fox said, praising him, "but why?"

"Yeah, exactly. Why exactly?"

"Because out of everybody in Zell, the two of them are the only ones that have never given a single schilling's tip."

But at that moment, the handless Frau turned to Andi. And that really took Brenner by surprise now. That the two of them knew each other.

"Lorenz is getting out today," she says.

"Out today, back in tomorrow," Andi says.

"I'm picking him up," Handless says.

"The ambulance picks him up. Then we pick him up. Then they pick him back up. Then we pick him back up, then—"

"Are you with me?" Handless says, because this blabber of Andi's, well, she wasn't having it one bit.

"Do you mean, do I understand what you're saying, or am I going where you're driving to: nuthouse!"

Handless had these thick glasses, the type that was fashionable in the seventies. And thick glasses like that, well, you don't see much of her face. Just her eyes, and those were twice as big as normal, because she must've been horribly farsighted.

With these enormous eyes of hers, she looks at Brenner now and asks him if maybe he'd like to come along. She says:

"I have to pick up my friend Lorenz Antretter from the hospital. He's being released today."

Now, Lorenz, that's Vergolder's nephew. And it was Lorenz, too, who'd provided Vergolder with his alibi for the night of the murder. Brenner tried to hide his surprise, though.

"You're here on your own anyway, walking," Handless says.

Of course, you couldn't not hear Brenner's amazement now when he said:

"But, can you drive a car?"

CHAPTER 5

Now, to pick up Lorenz Antretter. Needless to say, Brenner's interest was piqued. Vergolder was with Lorenz all evening long, December the twenty-first. That's when Lorenz gets his Christmas gift every year, always the twenty-first, because on the twenty-fourth, of course, just family.

Company Christmas with the ski school on the twenty-second, and with the lift personnel on the twenty-third. On the twenty-fourth, only the closest family, Vergolder's wife, if she were still alive, and her parents, who came over from America every year at Christmas. Kids, well, none, and since his wife died, only the in-laws. And last Christmas, needless to say, not even the in-laws anymore.

But this piqued Brenner's interest now, why Lorenz was getting picked up by Andi the Fox of all people. And frankly, even more than that, what interested him was how that's supposed to work, a woman with no hands driving a car.

But then, it was just like with the beer-drinking. I mean, so far as Brenner goes, it seemed more or less normal to him. There were these knobs mounted on the steering wheel—it almost looked like the wheel of a ship, of an ocean freighter. Like on TV, where the captain just stands and turns, that's how it looked, and the German wedged her arm-stumps between these knobs, and that's how she steered.

Naturally Brenner thought she'd have an automatic transmission, but not what you're thinking, her having an automatic transmission. She changed gears, that was a real thrill, because, on the gear stick some kind of cup had been screwed on, and she stuck her arm-stump into it, and that's how she changed gears.

And Brenner was amazed at how safe she drove. He didn't have much time to concern himself with Handless, though. Because Andi, who was sitting in the back, and Brenner was in the passenger seat, and from the backseat, Andi was telling him his tale, no interruptions.

Now, you should know, people say Andi's a little slow. And to Brenner, it seemed more like the gas jockey was a little too fast. But they meant the same thing, the people and Brenner.

"That alibi of Vergolder's, you do know it's a bunch of baloney, right, detective? A bunch of *Schmarren*?"

This struck the German as odd and she laughed into the rearview mirror now:

"*Schmarren* fit for a kaiser?"

"Nuthouse *Schmarren*," Andi says.

It seemed to Brenner like Andi's rage was spreading, like when you get a toothache today and a sore throat tomorrow, and the day after that it's a middle-ear infection. First, it started off on the asphalt with Gschwentner the farmer, then it caught Vergolder, and now Andi's rage wasn't even stopping at his friend Lorenz.

Brenner wasn't completely certain about that, though. It's more like when you get an infection that meanders around, practically aimless. Or, Andi's rage was like when you get yourself all charged up with electricity off a cow fence and then you shake somebody's hand, and then he shakes somebody else's hand, and the person who gets electrified isn't you but the last person in the chain. And the last in the chain, that was Andi's rage at Lorenz now.

"Why do you say nuthouse *Schmarren?*" Brenner says.

"Where are we picking Lorenz up from, Detective?"

"The nuthouse," Brenner says.

Interesting, though. Andi didn't want to hear that get repeated. Another person saying nuthouse about his friend Lorenz.

"It's not what you think, though," he says, "because Lorenz isn't nearly as bad as the other Zellers. Take Mario."

All of the sudden Mario was standing on the end of the cow-fence chain now.

"You know Mario, Detective?"

"Fürstauer's assistant."

"That's Mario. Every night he stops in to gas up his moped, his KTM. Always right as I'm closing up. And every day he only puts a liter in. So I says to Mario, he should kindly act like a normal person and gas up once a week, because why else does a moped tank hold five liters for, what do you think, Detective?"

"So that you can put five liters in it."

"Or four, as far as I'm concerned. Mario, though, he says to me: But this is a business, isn't it. So I says: This ain't a business, because I can scrape more off the bottom of my shoe!"

Brenner was immediately sorry that he laughed at that. Because, Andi, naturally:

"I can scrape more off the bottom of my shoe!"

And because nobody was laughing anymore, he got dissatisfied, and needless to say, one last time:

"I can scrape more off the bottom of my shoe!"

Brenner was amazed at how deft the German was on the road. A few times he even caught pedestrians staring, or other drivers looking over and desperately searching for her hands.

But try talking to the German, well, that was currently impossible.

"Interesting how you get the most tips when it's overcast. But not like you're thinking. Because certain kinds you never get tips from. Out of principle. Certain kinds of cars and certain kinds of drivers: never a tip. Interesting, though, how those kinds seem to multiply in certain kinds of weather. Nice weather, let's say. And on top of that, nice weather gets you the most bugs on the windshield. So you're washing off dead bodies. And bug bodies are the tiniest. But those blue-bloodsuckers. Because those are the kinds, like Vergolder, I never wash their windshields—out of principle. I'm always telling them that there's no point in weather like this because—too many blue-bloodsuckers out flying around. They get annoyed that I'm always telling them the same story. But they never seem to get it that it's them, I mean with the blue-bloodsuckers. Those tightwads theirselves is what I'm talking about, those tip-misers. Because, to be honest, the blue-bloodsuckers aren't the worst when it comes to cleaning. What's bad's the bee-eaters, they're big as birds—and that's just when they're squashed. But it's those tightwads theirselves I'm talking about when I say to them blue-bloodsuckers that there are too many blue-bloodsuckers around."

Andi got tired at some point, and by the time they got to the tunnel, he was asleep in the backseat.

"He's like a child," the German said.

"You got kids?" the detective asked.

But the car ahead of them, he must've been a crazy. Middle of the tunnel he peels out, crosses the double-lines, and overtakes a truck. This was the tunnel that just six months ago five people died in, all because somebody had the same idea. This time nothing happened, only the detective forgot that he'd just asked a question.

"Are you actually from Holland?"

Handless's German was so peculiar. Awkward, it sounded, or somehow, let's say, like when there's an opera on TV. Not just precise High German, but practically right angles. Just like the way High German sounds to us Austrians, maybe that's how Handless's language sounds to a High German. Somewhat stilted, the way people sound when they have a perfect command of a foreign language. And the fact that it's not their native language—you only notice it because they never make a mistake. So Brenner thought, Maybe she's Dutch.

"I'm from Hamburg."

And that's strange to our ears, too, of course, Hamburg German. Or the German they speak way up there, let's say, like that political guy up in Schleswig-Holstein, where they found him dead in the bathtub with his clothes on.

"But I've been living in Zell for more than a year now," she says.

"*Living* living here?" Brenner says.

"Do you know Preussenstadl?"

Of course Brenner knew Preussenstadl. It's a humongous apartment complex, built in the Alpine-chalet style, four floors, fifty-two apartments, pricey as sin—and almost all Germans who bought them up as vacation apartments.

"I'm a long-term visitor."

"Just like me."

"Yes, and like the old Americans, too. They were frequent visitors to Zell."

"Did you know them?"

"With Americans you can never know for sure if you know them."

"So you knew them well enough?"

"I speak passable English. And, well, we shared a mutual interest."

"Curling?"

"No, they had no interest whatsoever in curling."

The German needed her full concentration now in order to pass two semis on a bend in the autobahn. Then she said:

"Community theater."

"But they didn't know a word of German!"

"I don't always understand the dialect myself. Neverthe-less. We actually first met at a *Vormachen*."

"*Vormachen*? Now I'm the one that doesn't understand."

"You've never been to a *Vormachen*? You simply must! A lovely tradition. Whenever the next wedding is, you'll have to come with me to the *Vormachen*. The old Americans rarely left Vergolder's Castle to come down into the city. Eighty years old, after all. But they always made it to a *Vormachen* whenever they were in Zell. They just loved a good *Vormachen*."

"But what it is, this *Vormachen*, you're not going to tell me."

"Ah, *Vormachen*, it can't be explained," the German says and concentrates on the road.

Brenner could've cared less whether she explained what a *Vormachen* was or wasn't to him just now. Main thing, she doesn't drive into the car in front of them. That was his only concern right now.

"The bride and groom come out of the church, and on the church square, the locals perform a short theater scene for them. Anecdotes from the bride and groom's pasts. How the couple met. Very comical and often quite beautiful—well, trenchant, let's say. At every *Vormachen*, I laugh so hard I cry."

"And the Americans found it amusing, too."

"What do you mean amusing—every single time they would tell me about the *Vormachen* at their daughter's wed-ding to Vergolder Antretter from God knows how many years ago. You know how old people are always telling the same old story. Vergolder had been seriously offended at the time."

"Grooms are no fun."

"As I said, it's often rather pointed. And evidently, at the *Vormachen,* someone alluded to an affair between Vergolder and a nurse."

"And that amused the Americans, that their son-in-law was having a thing on the side with a nurse?"

"Not on the side. Earlier. Sins of youth. The old folks simply found the whole circus amusing."

"That's something right up the Americans' alleys. What with their five divorces all the time—a *Vormachen* for every one."

"No, no, Herr Detective, such sterotypes! They'd just celebrated their sixtieth wedding anniversary."

"Which you know all about."

Brenner almost would've preferred for Andi to wake up again now. Because the German had this bad habit. Purely insofar as, let's say, cars and drivers go. She always looked you right in the eye when she was talking to you. Now, normally, that's not necessarily uncomfortable. But in this case. She was hissing down the Autobahn at 130. And on top of that, well, no hands after all, even if she was a good driver, unbelievable, but still, just her two arm-stumps on the steering wheel. And when she was talking, she always took her eyes off the road and looked right at Brenner with those enormous eyes of hers. Because they were magnified so big by her farsighted glasses.

"It's quite lovely here," she says.

"Here in the tunnel?" Brenner says.

He was thinking, I'll make a joke, and if I make a joke, maybe I'll get her to look back at the road again, at least in the tunnel, because this here's a place with oncoming traffic. But, nothing doing, she didn't understand it was a joke, and Brenner, of course, ready with a stereotype: Germans, no sense of humor. She looked at him with her polyp eyes and said:

"No, here in Zell."

"You don't like it in Hamburg?"

"I do. Quite lovely. Quite lovely indeed. But everything moves very fast there. Whereas here, everything's allowed to move a tiny bit—just a *bisserl*—more slowly."

Needless to say, we're all the same down here. We don't like it when a German imitates our dialect. And it wasn't any different for Brenner, a *bisserl*. And then that bit about the "slowly," practically—well, it's true, of course, but we don't like hearing it. But Handless didn't mean it quite so generally, because now she says:

"Even the murders move more slowly down here. In Hamburg, shot on the spot. And here, deep frozen."

And then, she even laughed. Brenner thought: This I don't understand, either, what's so funny about that. But he didn't say anything.

Once they got there, they couldn't find the hospital porter at first. And then he couldn't find the shift nurse in charge. But don't get me wrong, everything was clean and well organized. Okay, maybe a little slow. Above all, the patients, of course—slowed down, I mean, for all practical purposes, medicated—they'd go strolling through the park with this vacant look about them. Because they've got a wonderful park there, and it was only just three o'clock now, glorious fall day, warm twenty-seven C, and so of course the patients were thinking, too: I'd better make the most of this while it lasts.

Lorenz wasn't there, though. Not at all. He'd just gotten picked up fifteen minutes ago. By his uncle, says the shift nurse.

Needless to say, Andi turned very pale now. And the German looked a little off, too. Because Lorenz only had one uncle. And that was Vergolder Antretter. And when the three of them had took off, from the curling strip, Vergolder had still been standing there on the asphalt.

CHAPTER 6

Two days later, as Brenner went trundling down the Schmit-
tenstrasse, it was the ninth of September already. It still
wasn't any cooler, and this *Altweibersommer*—Indian summer, I think you call it—had Zell bathed in a light that
would've made you think the mountains were right outside
your door.

And on top of that, there was music playing—okay, not
in reality. Brenner, his head, it had this tic somehow. All the
sudden some *Schlager* would pop up out of his memory, and
he couldn't get rid of it again. But not because he'd heard the
song somewhere, and that's why. No, all of the sudden, there
it was, out of nowhere. And pay attention now. Because if
Brenner had given any thought to how the words to this
song actually went, even though he was only humming the
melody to himself, then the words would've been an exact fit.
A fit with the situation he was presently stuck in.

And as he's walking into the post office now, he starts
humming it all over again, this French *chanson* that plagued
him all of yesterday. But not what you're thinking, now he's
finally sending his report off to the Meierling Detective
Agency. Because Brenner still hadn't wrote that yet.

The envelope he was mailing was just a private matter,

on account of his insurance, because that was all a lot more complicated now that he wasn't on the force anymore. Leni Bacher was sitting behind the counter, and Brenner was struck by how the stylish outfit she had on just served to highlight what a farmer's face she had.

Leni smiled at him knowingly, because she thought it was his report, and week in week out he'd handed his report to her to mail. And even to Brenner it seemed like she looked disappointed when she read the address, I mean, that the envelope was only going to the insurance company.

It was the same exact postage as it always was when Brenner mailed his report, though, and out of habit, Leni gave him a receipt for it. Brenner pocketed the receipt but he already knew that he'd lose it just like all the others. Nevertheless, only seven schillings fifty.

The song was still humming around in him when, as he was walking out, he stuck a ten in the Quick Draw. And then he had to turn right around again because he won something, ten schillings, and he could pick it right up from the lady back at the counter.

Standing in line in front of him was a businesswoman all made up and with a whole stack of payment slips. Now he was going to have to wait a few minutes for his ten, and that melody was going through his head again—I'm talking a real earworm, even though, so far as the melody goes, it wasn't an earworm at all.

Then he throws the ten he just won back into the Quick Draw, and he was glad he didn't win anything this time, because this way, at least, he wouldn't have to go back in there again. And actually he should've been on Bahnhofstrasse some time ago, in Perterer's gun shop, because yesterday he hadn't been able to decide.

But today I need to make a decision, Brenner thought, and there's that old malady of his. That he couldn't make up his mind. And maybe that's why he spent so long fooling around with the Quick Draw before he finally made his way over to the Zell gun shop.

And needless to say, the melody, right back in there again. The first time went like this for him: so, Brenner, just sixteen, and his first girlfriend runs out on him. For days there was a melody going through his head, some kind of American church song is what it was, and dammit if he didn't hate that song. Well, best case, like a pimple that you pop. But he just couldn't get rid of it. It's this—eh, maybe you know it: "Nobody knows the trouble," in other words, a self-pity song.

But please, at least that's a popular song. This time, though, it was a song that Brenner only heard once his whole life. The French teacher played it for them in school because she always schlepped some ancient record player to their last class before Christmas and played *chansons* for them. Georges Moustaki, Brenner still knew it to this day. He sang:

"Rien n'a changé, mais pourtant tout est different."

And really, nothing's really changed. There wasn't anything new for Brenner to know—anything, let's say, that you could play up as news in a ten-line summary. And yet. All the sudden everything was different now.

Vergolder picking up his nephew—that just didn't want to enter Brenner's skull. When everybody in Zell knew for a fact that Lorenz outright hated his uncle. That's what made Vergolder's alibi so watertight, that it came from Lorenz. And now at curling, Vergolder sees Brenner driving off with the German to pick up Lorenz, doesn't make a peep, and then races out himself so that they can't catch him.

"*Rien n'a changé, mais pourtant tout est différent*" sang over and over again in Brenner's head, as he walked to the gun shop, more or less on autopilot. Because guns are a real problem, of course. Especially when you've been used to one for twenty years. Since Brenner had left the force, he'd left his gun, too, of course. And what kind of a detective doesn't have a gun.

Now, maybe you know Zell's local gun dealer on Bahnhofstrasse. Perterer. Perterer Jr. Because Perterer Sr.—a tragic story. But that wasn't the first businessman who got noodled up in a tax audit. But these days if it's a tobacconist or a baker that gets caught, well, they don't have any dangerous goods in their shops. Practically speaking, they can't point their wares at themselves. So they sleep on it, and the next day they don't kill themselves anymore, taxes or no taxes.

But with a gun dealer, of course. It was the Smith & Wesson with Perterer Sr. But that was a full year ago now, still before Brenner's time.

Perterer was studying in Paris at the time of that tragic business with his father. Languages he studied. Now he had to return home, take over the business. True, he wasn't as interested in guns, but his mother, all alone back home, and so he said to himself, Why should I keep traipsing up and down the boulevards of Paris when I could have a trim gun shop back home. And about the taxes, the mayor helped him out a little because—a young man, the Zellers said, we'll help him out a little.

"Have you made up your mind?" Perterer Jr. asked the moment Brenner walked into the shop. Because this was Brenner's fourth time in there now.

"I don't know," he said, and that was the truth, because he was still torn between three different models, all of which had their advantages.

"Just take your time," Perterer Jr. says, because he was anything but a pushy salesman, very different from his father. But Brenner almost wished that Perterer Jr. would in fact put a little pressure on him now, because he just couldn't decide on his own.

"I'm just about thinking I'll take the Walther."

"The Walther, yes, you can't go wrong there."

"Although, it's not doing anything for me."

"It's a matter of taste, of course."

"It's the grip I don't like."

"Well, when it comes to the grip, it's a matter of taste."

"The barrel I do like."

"Top-notch barrel."

"The grip, though."

"Then, get the Smith and Wesson, it's got a nice grip."

But not because Perterer Jr. was trying to talk Brenner into the more expensive Smith & Wesson. Brenner had been going around in circles for weeks now, should I get the Walther or the Smith & Wesson.

"Or you could take the Glock out one more time for me."

Without a hint of impatience, Perterer Jr. took the Glock out of the display case.

"Nice and light, the Glock," Brenner says.

"And the precision."

"Do you think I should get the Glock?"

"The American cops are using the Glock now, too."

"Yeah, maybe I'll get the Glock," Brenner says but sets the Glock back down on Perterer Jr.'s shop counter.

But not what you're thinking, that Brenner had something against guns, as a matter of principle. In his own quiet way, he was even a good shot. Officially, he'd never shot anybody. Übung *Spitze*, though, that's this breathing technique. Because Brenner once let a yoga teacher show him this breathing technique on account of his headaches. For shooting, though, a tremendous advantage.

"Maybe I'll stop back one more time this evening for a look," Brenner says to Perterer Jr. and then hurries on his way. He just wasn't in the right frame of mind to make a selection right now. What he needed was to go to the Feinschmeck. But today it wasn't Erni the waitress that was drawing him to the Feinschmeck.

In the fifties, the Feinschmeck must've been the most fashionable restaurant for miles around. As Brenner entered the restaurant now, his gaze fell first on the instruments from the dance band that played there three nights a week, because that's the way it's always been, that there's music at the Feinschmeck. But needless to say, Brenner didn't need any more of that.

"*Rien n'a changé, mais pourtant tout est different*" started right back up in his mind at just the sight of the instruments.

The Feinschmeck was practically empty. Only the *tarock* players were here, of course, and at another table an old woman was sitting and reading a magazine with a magnifying glass. And way back in the next room that was otherwise completely empty, Lorenz Antretter was waiting for him.

Brenner knew him from having seen him around but had never spoke with him. Lorenz was roughly Brenner's age. But you couldn't imagine two guys that were more different.

"Have you been waiting long?" Brenner asks.

Lorenz nodded. He was so thin that Brenner wondered how he could even hold his head up.

"No. Ten minutes."

Now, either Lorenz was a chain smoker or he was very nervous, because in the ashtray there were already four cigarette butts. And if he was nervous, then was it on account of Brenner, or was he just always that way.

"How are you?" Brenner asks and then takes a seat vis-à-vis Lorenz.

Lorenz does this movement for a second time now, maybe on account of Brenner wondering how he could even hold his head up. It starts out first as a nod, except the only difference is that his head doesn't come back up. And that's the precise moment when he'd sweep his blond curls off his forehead—or were they more white? Right in the middle, you couldn't really say.

Interesting, though. The next time he does this, he nods just like before and leaves his head down again. So, somehow he has to get his head surreptitiously back up, because how else can he start the next downward nod if not from the up-beat again.

"What're we having?" Erni the waitress asks.

Lorenz already had a glass of club soda sitting on the table, so it was clear that the "we" only applied to Brenner. It was always when Erni didn't quite know how she should address a customer that she talked to them like this.

A few days earlier she'd addressed Brenner with this "we" for the first time. And Brenner seized the opportunity right away, because he played dumb and asked the waitress, does that mean you'll be joining me for a drink. So, she had to knock back a glass on Brenner's dime. And maybe that's why she was grinning so cheekily now when she said:

"What're we having?"

"A beer," Brenner says, even though, normally he wouldn't drink beer this time of day.

"Thanks for taking the time," he says to Lorenz, and Lorenz does his half nod again, sweeps his curls off his forehead and takes a drag on his cigarette.

"You know why I want to speak with you."

Lorenz, again, with the half-nod.

"Did you know the victims very well?"

"No thanks," Lorenz says.

"And with your uncle, you don't have the best relation-ship, either."

Pause. Then Lorenz says slowly:

"Why are you asking? If you already know."

"But why were you with him, then, on the night of De-cember twenty-first?"

Pause. Now it was slowly dawning on Brenner that the medication from the psychiatric clinic hadn't exactly made Lorenz any quicker.

"How often am I supposed to explain this exactly?"

"One more time," Brenner says.

"Every year I go to my uncle's on December twenty-first. That's my Christmas."

"On the twenty-first?"

"Yes. Because the twenty-third's my uncle's company Christmas, ski school, I mean. Gondolas on the twenty-second. And family on the twenty-fourth."

"When did your father die?"

"That was when he was exactly as old as I am now, that's when he died."

Lorenz appeared completely emotionless to Brenner—that, too, must've been the meds, and that's why, without giving it a second thought, Brenner asked him:

"And what did he die of?"

"Don't know."

"You don't want to talk about it?"

Lorenz gave another half-nod and fished the next ciga-rette out of his pack. Then he says:

"Lung cancer."

Says Brenner:

"How old were you at the time?"

Says Lorenz:

"Thirteen."

Says Brenner:

"And who was your guardian, then?"

Says Lorenz:

"My uncle."

Says Brenner:

"So, is Vergolder your uncle on your father's side or your mother's side?"

Says Lorenz:

"Both sides. He's my uncle on both sides."

Says Brenner:

"Now, that you're going to have to explain to me."

Says Lorenz:

"My father wasn't my biological father. Because I never knew my biological father. And my mother disappeared. After my birth, I mean. Probably in the lake, people say. That's why I don't swim. I've never gone swimming in the lake. That's why people think I'm crazy. One time I did go swimming. At night. In the winter, though. Nearly drowned. But my father was still alive at the time. I caused him a lot of worry. My father died of worry, you know."

Says Brenner:

"Your adoptive father."

Says Lorenz:

"If you like, sure, my adoptive father."

Says Brenner:

"Why did he take you in?"

Says Lorenz:

"He was my uncle. I had two uncles. Two brothers of my mother's. One of them took me in."

Says Brenner:

"But the two brothers didn't get along very well."

Says Lorenz:

"Hated, you might say."

Says Brenner:

"What kind of work did your father do?"

Says Lorenz:

"My father helped my uncle with his gilding. He was an actual *Vergolder*. Church painter. Didn't have any time for gilding, though. So, he trained my father to."

Says Brenner:

"And you? What's your trade?"

Says Lorenz:

"I helped my father with his gilding."

Says Brenner:

"And how do you support yourself today?"

Says Lorenz:

"Vergolder is a parasite. Parasite on society. And I am a parasite on Vergolder."

Says Brenner:

"Why did you give your uncle a false alibi, then, if you think so little of him?"

Says Lorenz:

"Hate, you might say."

Says Brenner:

"Okay, let's say hate."

Says Lorenz:

"Because I have an appreciation for him. I appreciate him, I do. On December twenty-first, I go to his house. There, I always get a passbook to a savings account."

Says Brenner:

"And why didn't you go up to his place this year, then, of all years? And why did you testify that you were up there with him?"

Lorenz gestured to Erni to bring him another club soda. And Brenner knew, of course, that the best way to recognize an alcoholic is by their constant seltzer-ordering. He took a slug of beer to give Lorenz time. Maybe, somewhere along his convoluted way, he'll find an answer to my question after all, Brenner thought.

"All that about the nervous breakdown, I explained it to my uncle," says Lorenz.

Says Brenner:

"You had a nervous breakdown?"

Says Lorenz:

"The mountains' nervous breakdown. The people will see. In December, they'll see."

Says Brenner:

"What's in December?"

Says Lorenz:

"You're in for a surprise."

Says Brenner:

"Me?"

Says Lorenz:

"No, all you people."

Says Brenner:

"And what kind of a surprise?"

Says Lorenz:

"It upset my father that I was so excited about gilding. At first he wanted me to help him, but then it upset him. Because I was only helping him because he couldn't manage the work alone anymore. But he didn't mean for me to get so into it. I was just, let's say, nine or ten years old. Vergolder had a souvenir shop, maybe you know it, *Rieder* it's called, but Vergolder owns it.

My father taught me about nature. He used to like to draw. We all have a talent for painting—grandfather, too, a church painter. But he had no choice but to gild. Kids and so on. But now, he was teaching me about nature. Because he saw right away that I have talent. Then, when he took me into the souvenir business because he couldn't manage the work alone anymore, he was disappointed. Since I was crazy about the gilding, and even about the souvenir business, too. Because I was still just a kid, and I liked all that *Klimbim*.

And the drawing, maybe he was too strict with me. He always said, you don't need gold because the landscape glows all on its own. When I was a child I didn't really understand that, of course.

Also, the real gold is just fool's gold, my father says in his hoarse voice, because that was the lung cancer already, but we didn't know it yet. I didn't understand about the fool's gold.

At first he took me to work with him, and then, I just

couldn't understand it, not yet. My father says, the landscape glows all on its own. If you only look at it long enough, then you can feel its nerves. I didn't understand what that was supposed to mean, though, that you could feel the landscape's nerves.

I only felt my own nerves. Why would the gold suddenly stop glowing, I wondered, if I'd seen it glowing. Everything in the souvenir shop gleamed, even the schoolgirls' lipstick cases and the cigarette holders gleamed. Only the landscape didn't. After my father died, I slowly began to feel like the mountains were getting more and more nervous."

It often works this way that a person is sometimes thinking about things, and right at the wrong moment— something completely incongruous. And now Brenner was briefly entertaining what Meierling, well, his boss, I should say, because, Meierling wasn't his real name, just the agency was called Meierling, his name was Brugger. What Brugger would make of this, how he would take what Lorenz was saying and put it into a ten-line summary.

Lorenz was already lighting one cigarette off the other, and Brenner took advantage of the break now to ask one more time:

"What'll happen in December?"

Lorenz says: "When I was little, my father always called the mountains elephants. Then, they started cutting the forest down. To make way for the ski lifts. But when there weren't any more leaves withering along the elephants' backs, then it was like when somebody takes a rheumatoid arthritis blanket made of dry leaves and yanks it off you."

Now, Brenner could've made light of this and swept the whole thing off the table as pure craziness. But, on the other hand, he thought, it's not all that different, what Lorenz is saying here and what you read everyday in the papers. And so he didn't lose his patience and asked:

"What'll the people be surprised about come December?"

And Lorenz says: "When the rheumatoid arthritis blanket gets yanked off of them, the mountains will begin to tremble in order to warm themselves again. Not noticeably, not so much that you'd notice. Only the dam walls will feel it. The Limberg Dam and the Drossen Dam. And the Mooser Dam. One and a half million cubic meters of concrete. The Symbol of the Republic. Indestructible. When the mountains begin to tremble, the dam walls will break away from their holdings. The dam waters will flood the Zell basin—a full meter high—and twenty thousand people will drown. Because it'll happen so fast, they won't even have time to think."

Lorenz ordered another club soda from the waitress now, even though the glass in front of him was still half-full. And once Erni was out of earshot, Brenner says:

"And that will happen this December?"

Lorenz says: "No, no. In December we're putting on our play. Andi and the German. And Clare."

"And you."

"And me."

CHAPTER 7

When it comes to Saturdays, it's a big deal. Not always easy for people to bear, Saturdays. For Brenner, it wasn't much different. Two days after meeting Lorenz, he was sitting right back at the Feinschmeck. Seemed to him like he'd been sitting here the whole time, though, and was only just now leaving.

As Brenner walked out of the Feinschmeck, Zell appeared more deserted than ever before to him. But there was something else different about it now, too. Because what a Saturday means to the course of a week, let's say, well, that's what the end of a season is to the course of a year. In Zell, anyway, that's how it is. So far as desertedness goes. And as Detective Brenner's walking down the street, he realizes now, even before the automatic door-closer can draw the door to the Feinschmeck shut: end of a season and a Saturday, at the same time.

What more do you need. Brenner crossed the church square that was normally teeming with tourists. But, now, not a single tourist on the Kirchplatz. Only a few old ladies, he saw, as they flitted into church. And because it was the end of a season and the end of a week at the same time, he simply followed them into the church.

Or was it also on account of that thing that Lorenz had told him about two days ago. Exactly the same as what Andi had told him. That they'd been rehearsing with the community theater. That they'd be performing it in December. That that's why he hadn't actually been at Vergolder's. But in a play that was about Vergolder. And how surprised people would be when they performed the play in December. Lorenz and Andi. And the German, in effect, the director.

And, then, this girl that Lorenz had mentioned. Clare Corrigan, not her real name at all, she simply went by that. Brenner had noticed her around Zell here and there. Because one thing you can't forget. In a big city, nobody gets excited when an adolescent behaves provocatively these days. But, in a small town, another story altogether. Needless to say, Clare, with her painted incisor, not to be overlooked in Zell.

But that's how it is in the provinces, Brenner thought. Either the people don't care at all about the trendy stuff that's so important in the cities. Or, they don't waste any time going overboard with it. Mail-ordering the unhealthiest fads that can only be found in the *Quelle* catalogue. And pyelitis, that's out. He knew that one all too well from growing up in Puntigam. Jimi Hendrix must've been on TV all of once. And the very next morning, guaranteed, the police found a drug O.D. in the bathroom at the train station.

In the church now, Brenner started brooding. He hadn't been to church more than two or three times in the last twenty years. Now he was remembering his sister's first wedding, she married a real showboat, wore a white suit to their wedding, needless to say, divorce soon after, what can I tell you. And then, two and a half years ago, the funeral for his colleague Schmeller, who, during the bank robbery at the, uh, the, where was that now—well, he lost his life. And by a shot to the neck, no less, but that was a damned stupid coincidence, bad luck on both their parts, Schmeller and the bank robber, because he'd meant to shoot into the air, that was obvious.

Tunzinger was the one on duty there in Oberndorf— right, at the Raiffeisen Bank in Oberndorf, that's it. And at the memorial service for Schmeller, he whispers to Brenner that it'd been a mistake. But, in front of the judge, natu- rally, he keeps his mouth shut. There's no two ways around it, murder of a cop—needless to say, nobody wanted to hear any different.

That was, like I said, two and a half years ago. But, the fact that the ceremony at the church there in Zell seemed so familiar to Brenner now—because he could practically predict the priest's every move—that had nothing to do with Schmeller's funeral. No, because, as a boy, he'd been an altar boy. Back in his elementary school days in Puntigam, Brenner, always the diligent server—often every day, even— and so on account of that, of course, he still remembered everything, because in church, things don't exactly change with the seasons.

Even the sexton in Zell was every bit as withered and ageless a little man as they'd had in Puntigam. And just like in Puntigam, he would float soundlessly through the sanctuary shortly before the mass was to begin so that he could light the candles. That hadn't changed one bit—technological revolution or no technological revolution, the Zell sexton did it exactly like the Puntigam sexton had did it forty years ago. A two-meter-long pole with a wick at the end so that he could get to everywhere, and next to the wick was this little helmet-like thing—cone-shaped, I mean—and after mass he'd put the candles out with it.

Now, there were reforms, of course, sixties, let's say, under Johannes, that was the pope at the time, the twenty-third, and he brought about a lot of these reforms, a real butchers' council. But, thirty years later, you still wouldn't have noticed them much in Zell. Take women. It used to be that the women sat on the left and the men on the right. When Brenner was just a wee pip of an altar boy, this was still totally normal. In Zell, though, this was still normal, more or less.

On the women's side, at least, Brenner didn't see a single man. Conversely, on the men's side, it was almost completely empty. A few boys, and two, three old men, nothing else. Brenner stayed in the back and stood by the entrance, just like the men used to like to do, because, that way, during the sermon, they could sneak out to the bar.

But once the mass began, Brenner knelt in the last empty pew on the men's side. He was struck by the fact that the two altar boys were girls, in other words, against the rules, and that the priest, flanked by the two altar girls, walked out of the sacristy way too fast. He was more like your small spry type, the Zell priest, and it really did look as if he ran, more or less, out of the sacristy—you'd have thought you could hear the chasuble flapping, but that's the way he always did it.

The congregation rises, but Brenner doesn't stand up, no, the opposite, hunkers right down into his pew. Maybe you're familiar with this: half-sitting, half-kneeling, head buried in hands. And at the same time, of course, in your head, some-where else completely, just not at church.

For months he'd been gathering everything, the most trivial facts, all of it compiled with conscientiousness. And now, for the first time, he actually had something substantial. Vergolder's false alibi, right in Brenner's hands all the sud-den. Success, you'd like to believe. But no, everything inside Brenner was resisting him taking it too seriously.

Maybe it was the smell of the candles in the church, the incense. And the prayers that the congregation recited in chorus, and the pictures of the saints, and the church hymnals, and the voice of the priest echoing out of the tinny church loudspeaker. Say what you will, but it had a certain something to it. Maybe that's why Brenner started feeling twinges of a more or less moral nature now.

Now, don't get me wrong. Because, these days, a lot of talk about methods gets bandied around all the time. Brenner, of course, his method was to devote himself to all of the details, and so he didn't make any distinctions along the lines of important or un-. But that's not really a method. That was just because—that's just how Brenner was and didn't know any different.

And now, as he noticed how out-of-place it felt for him

to be served such an enormous piece of evidence all the sudden, Brenner took stock of himself—you'd have thought, Old Testament.

Had this not always been his biggest failing? Was this not why his life had gotten onto the wrong track? Everything always too complicated. Always getting everything from god knows how far. Not like a normal person simply does, with whatever's closest at hand.

"Sex, and I'll say it again, sex!" the priest said into the microphone now, because the Zell priest liked to preach about topics like this, and it startled Brenner a moment, surprised him that the priest was already on the sermon now—practically half an hour gone by, and here he'd thought, five minutes.

While he was loafing there with his head in his hands, you might've thought, a proper believer, you know, praying or suffering. And somehow, that's how it was, too. It wasn't really the case of the two Americans that had him preoccupied, but his own case. His own inability. That he's always so unable to tell the essential apart from the inessential.

"People today worship at the altar of sex."

He used to think maybe it was an asset. Not as much judgment, as it were. Until at some point he realized that it just made him utterly, I don't know. Unable to cope with life. By that point it was more or less too late already. When he noticed that people like Nemec aren't interested in the truth at all.

"Even in kindergarten, the teachers are talking about sex already."

People like Nemec are only looking for solutions, Brenner thought. And often enough they'll find one. This wasn't the first time that Brenner thought this. But this time it wasn't Nemec but himself who he was taking to task. Because everything within him was struggling against the thought of Vergolder.

Then he heard the church pews creaking, and he knew that the sermon was over. The believers rose for the Creed, because he still knew that after the sermon comes the Creed, you don't forget a thing like that. But Brenner stayed huddled in his sufferer's stance; it seemed comfortable to him somehow. And it was cold in the church, too, still warm outside, but inside, cold as hell, and if you're huddled up like that, needless to say, it's warmer.

"I believe in God," the priest began chanting, and then, the believers, too, in chorus:

"the father almighty,
    creator of heaven and earth,
    I believe in Jesus Christ,
    his only son, our Lord."

There weren't all that many believers, just a pitiful little band of old, spent voices, rattling out the prayer:

"I believe in the Holy Spirit,
    the holy catholic church,
    the communion of saints,
    the forgiveness of sins,

the resurrection of the body,
and life everlasting. Amen."

And that's when it started in on Brenner again. He knew it from puberty, but it was still that way now. Now, this shouldn't sound somehow, you know. But he was seized by this incredible friskiness now, just like he always used to get—he barely had to see the inside of a church.

Back then, he believed it was connected to him having to go to mass—with the requiredness of it. But now, even though he was there voluntarily, nevertheless. Or sometimes, too, he thought, it was connected more to the body, you know, feeling confined, immobile, just unnatural, because a church pew like that, you're in there kneeling like you're in a vise. Or, more psychological, he thought, as in, the church wants to suppress sex, so now nature's fighting back.

Anyway, it had gotten to that point again. Thirty years later, and not the slightest bit of change. This had Brenner not quite wanting to believe it, but that's how it was. Before the priest even got started on the transubstantiation. And how, right at the transubstantiation, the altar girl on the left was ringing her handbell—it was like with those dog experiments, I don't know if you've ever heard about this, so, a bell rings when the dog gets a sausage, and soon it's gotten to the point that the ringing alone is enough, and the dog comes running with his mouth watering. Russian dogs, that's it.

And at that moment, where the altar girl's ring-a-linging and the priest's raising the chalice up in the air, who should pop up before Brenner's third eye, so to speak, the young schoolteacher, Kati Engljähringer.

Now, you should know—and so that you don't go thinking god knows what about Brenner—after all, it'd been three-quarters of a year that he'd been living alone in Zell. A man in his prime, you might say. And that thing with Betty, with the American insurance agent, that'd been a few weeks ago already. Besides, it surprised him, too, but for some reason he'd never quite coveted Betty. Maybe just because it was all too easy, what with their rooms right next door to each other. And if he was honest with himself, it was only in retrospect that he'd taken any real delight in it, once he realized that Mandl the reporter had been after her.

"This is my body," the priest was saying now, and maybe it was his sex sermon, too, that had Brenner unable to think about anything else. All of the sudden, Engljähringer seemed like the prettiest woman he'd ever seen in his whole life. But just between us: he thought that about just about any woman who had dark brown hair but skin so milky white, so translucent, that you don't see the freckles until you're two centimeters away.

But, then again, maybe it was only because this investigation had Brenner in a bit of a pickle. That he didn't know where to begin with Vergolder's false alibi. Maybe that was the reason why Brenner was feeling like a fifteen-year-old, I mean, where life's just about worn you down with its crap. And so it was the warm white skin of schoolteacher Kati Engljähringer that occurred to him. She first started out just doing her student-teaching here, and then she stuck around, or the school board wouldn't let her go anymore, so she must've been about twenty-seven already.

Right next to the church entrance are two phone booths, and that's where he was looking up Kati Engljähringer's number now. Then he almost didn't dare dial, but then he did after all. He was just glad that Lorenz had delivered this pretext right to him. Like I said, he was a bit of a coward in this regard, queasy in the stomach, you know, as he listened to it ring for the first time.

"This is Kati."

Her voice sounded so chummy that Brenner immediately feared she'd been waiting for a different call.

"This is Brenner. I'm a private detective working on the Parson case."

Now, normally, you'd expect some kind of reaction. But some people simply have this impossible habit. They fall silent on the phone exactly like if you were having a conversation with them face to face, as if it were the same thing. Needless to say, Brenner was getting a little frantic, and he noticed right away, too, how nervous his voice was sounding as he prattled on:

"I might have a few questions about a student. I can't explain it to you in any detail at the moment. I've received a tip about a student of yours. Maybe you could help me further. It doesn't concern the student herself. It's just—it would be great if I could speak with someone about her."

"Which student is it, then?"

"Clare Corrigan. I believe she goes by a different name, though."

"Yes, Elfi. She's not one of my students, though."

"Oh."

He was hoping she hadn't heard that just now. The disappointment in his voice. Through the phone booth window he looked out onto the church square. It was Saturday afternoon. End of the season. This time the pause in the conversation was on his dime. But just as he was about to end the conversation, she says:

"I had her last year in German. Maybe I can be helpful to you. Just come by."

"You mean—right now?"

"If you have time."

The schoolteacher lived in a *garçonnière* between the Schüttdorferstrasse and the lake. If you walk along the lake, it's only ten minutes from the church. The lake and the air and everything was so still now that you'd have thought the Saturday mood had infected even the weather.

Except Brenner. Needless to say, he was the exact opposite now. Mood, practically euphoric.

"I didn't realize you were a doctor," he said, when she opened the apartment door to him, because on the bell it said, "Dr. Engljähringer."

Her smile got under his skin, boy, I don't need to tell you. She had on a dark red knit dress, but it stopped a good half a meter above the knee. Brenner had to watch out that he didn't start breathing too heavily now.

"Have a seat," Engljähringer says, and points to the sectional, which faced not the lake but the Schüttdorferstrasse. The noise-reduction windows were an absolute necessity because the through-traffic never let up, not even on a Saturday.

On the coffee table was a composition book, and Brenner read the name off it:

"Elfi Lohninger. German. Sixth grade."

Engljähringer says, "You do know that Clare Corrigan's real name is actually Elfi Lohninger."

"What?"

Brenner's real thoughts were actually somewhere else. He was only looking at the schoolbook to keep from gawking at the red knit dress.

"Ah, yes, of course," Brenner says now. That was true, too. He really did know that already. But did Engljähringer the schoolteacher actually believe that that's why he'd come here.

"Would you like something to drink?"

"Are you having something?"

"If you'll have something."

The schoolteacher only had amaretto. Now, you should know, Brenner's grandmother back in Puntigam had always told him this story about sweet schnapps. Namely, how it was responsible for her bringing an illegitimate child into the world. Which, of course, was Brenner's mother. Because the master carpenter, her, a couple of sweet schnapps. Dispensed, as it were. Needless to say, this was seeming like a good sign to Brenner now, an auspicious beginning. And she had music, too, Engljähringer the schoolteacher. Adriano Celentano. Greatest Hits.

But that doesn't necessarily mean anything, of course.

Maybe she just loved Italy, they're all the same when it comes to that. Even looked a little Italian. Dark hair, light skin. Translucent freckles.

The schoolteacher told him stories about Elfi, i.e. Clare, that were more or less interesting for a good hour's worth. More or less interesting because Brenner didn't exactly know how interesting—watching her mouth while she talked, but like I said.

Brenner got to Engljähringer's shortly before eight. And now it was already past nine. Outside, pitch black.

"Will you have another?" Engljähringer the schoolteacher says. Offers an encouraging smile. But this was already his third now. And her third. Maybe a good sign, Brenner thought.

"You do know how people talk, that Clare is, how do they put it so nicely here? A *Nebenzu*," the schoolteacher says.

"A *Nebenzu?*"

"An illegitimate child of Vergolder's."

Now, though. A *Nebenzu*. Brenner didn't let anything show. Except for pouring himself another amaretto STAT:

"He seems, so, all over the place—"

He noticed that he was slurring his speech now. Because he'd had a beer earlier at the Feinschmeck.

"He seems, so, all over the place—somehow's got his finger in every pie."

Nine oh-seven is what time it was. Needless to say, Brenner wasn't looking at his watch. Because, then, maybe

Engljähringer would ask him if he needed to leave. But on the VCR behind Engljähringer he saw that it was nine oh-seven. Now, in the next fifteen minutes, something had to happen, one way or another.

And it just had to be the mention of Vergolder at just that moment that rattled Brenner. Just had to start thinking of Vergolder instead of Engljähringer. With his finger in every pie, just had to go thinking. Engljähringer must've noticed, though, that Brenner was having a problem, because she was smiling so nicely at him now. Or did it just seem that way to Brenner on account of the four or five amarettos.

"You could be in the pictures for pearly whites," he says now.

But just before this, you could hear a car pulling up and parking in front of the building, and now somebody was ringing Engljähringer's doorbell.

"That's just my boyfriend," Engljähringer the school-teacher says. She had dark hair, white skin with translucent freckles, and blue eyes with white flecks in them, roughly like a Bavarian check table cloth.

Just her boyfriend.

Brenner rated that as a bad sign. And then, all of the sudden, as Engljähringer was going into the foyer to let her boyfriend in, Brenner got a real panic-stricken feeling. Maybe this, too, was from the amaretto. Suddenly Brenner feared that it was Vergolder. That he'd turn out to be Engljähringer's lover.

Brenner couldn't have imagined anything worse just then. But then, it did get worse.

He heard her boyfriend's voice, but he didn't recognize it. And then he heard how the schoolteacher gave him a kiss hello. And then he came in. And then, it was Mandl the local reporter. But it took all his might for Brenner to keep himself from breathing too heavily, this time from rage.

CHAPTER 8

As Brenner took the narrow mountain road up to Vergolder's the next morning, his thoughts were still on Mandl: how Mandl's tie seemed even greener than the last time he'd seen him. Even though, by that point, only two candles were still burning in Engljähringer's living room. And that must've had something to do with how red Mandl's face was, because red and green, needless to say, a nice contrast.

"What are you looking for here!" Mandl shouted.

And Brenner says softly: "I look everywhere, Mandl."

"You look everywhere. But you don't find anything."

"You know what I'd like to find? You, with your mouth shut."

"My mouth, eh? I'm supposed to keep my mouth shut again. Give Vergolder my best. Tell him I've been keeping my mouth shut for a long time now. How come you got kicked off the force."

The schoolteacher was trying hard—damage control, as it were. She tried to calm Mandl down. But it was already out. And now, on his way to Vergolder's, Brenner still couldn't make heads or tails of it.

Why would Vergolder shield him. And if the police

considered Vergolder a suspect, why wouldn't the *Pinzgauer Post* write about it. That must've pleased Vergolder. And especially since it wasn't Brenner, wasn't his idea, but Nemec, it was his thing, the suspicion about Vergolder.

That last stretch before you get to Vergolder's is so steep that Brenner had to stop a couple times. Twelfth of September, and already so warm at this hour of the morning that you immediately break out in a sweat.

And Brenner didn't like it one bit when he had to do anything strenuous in the morning. Because his time of day didn't really begin until the afternoon. Two, three o'clock, that was Brenner's kind of time. But now, as he arrived at the parking lot in front of the Vergolder castle, he looked at his watch, and it seemed a little uncanny to him for a second there. Because nine oh-seven. It had been practically twelve hours exactly, on the dot, since Mandl had turned up at Engljähringer's apartment.

But it wasn't Mandl who was ringing a doorbell unannounced today, no, it was Brenner. And if, say, Mandl had been surprised twelve hours earlier, then it was Brenner who was surprised now, though not unpleasantly. He couldn't quite believe that Vergolder answers his own door.

You've got to picture it, the place looked like some grand manor house—if a proper butler had been standing in the doorway, that would've surprised Brenner less. Or, let's say, a maid at least. But not so, just Vergolder himself standing there, blue tracksuit, and says:

"Grüss Gott!"

"Maybe I should have called ahead," Brenner says. A bad

conscience suddenly grabbed hold of him because Vergolder was being so friendly.

"I'm not in the phone book," Vergolder says. And now he looks Brenner deep in the eyes. Because Vergolder, he was the type of guy—now how should I explain this to you. He liked to look at a person in this way that would've made you think, Here comes his most profound life lesson—Vergolder's gold, as it were. And that was exactly how he had his gaze trained on Brenner now, like the coach of a kids' soccer team, let's say, who says to his mini-men: "And one thing you must never, ever, forget!"

And after a few seconds Vergolder says:

"Believe it or not. Costs two-hundred and seventeen schillings not to get in the phone book."

For a moment Brenner didn't know what he should say to that, but Vergolder had already turned halfway around, and he says perfectly straight now, I mean, not as kindly, not with this kindhearted look of the kids' coach, but perfectly straight:

"Frankly, I've been expecting a visit from you."

But Brenner couldn't get Vergolder's eyes out of his mind now.

He'd had to deal with Vergolder twice when he was a cop, and really, Vergolder looked the same as ever. But that's exactly what it was. It wasn't anything strange that was bothering Brenner, no, but something familiar about his face.

Maybe some imperceptible resemblance to his nephew Lorenz. But how's that work, two more different types you can barely imagine. On the one hand, Vergolder, who, at seventy, was still bursting with energy and entrepreneurial verve. His snowy white hair, his tanned ski instructor's face, his squinty millionaire's eyes. On the other hand, and nearly a generation younger, Lorenz, with those resigned old eyes of his.

And then the house. If you can even call it a house. Castle more like, a few hundred meters above the lake, and from up here you could see the whole lake and the whole city of Zell.

But inside, how should I put it, you'd almost be disappointed. Given the outside, you would've expected more. They'd renovated the castle to such an extent that you'd have thought you were in a civil service apartment. And maybe, in the end, it'd struck Vergolder that way, too. Because Brenner was thinking now, Maybe that's why he's got so much old furniture stuffed into this place, so that it doesn't look like a civil service apartment from all the renovating. Because wherever he looked, Brenner saw a heap of antique furniture.

And as Vergolder led him further into the castle, there got to be more and more antique furniture. It was almost too much for Brenner. He had to look where he was going, make sure he was following Vergolder exactly, because everywhere he looked, he was stepping over a Madonna or a saint, he had to pay attention that he didn't step on anything.

Now, you should know, Brenner had a terrible sense of direction. And this, after twenty years on the force. You'd like to think a person might come to learn a thing like that, but no dice. Typically, all it takes is two turns, and he doesn't know where he is anymore—I mean, no talk of directions. And as Vergolder dragged him through a few hallways and up two, three staircases full of antiquities, needless to say, he immediately lost all sense of orientation.

But then, he knew where he was all over again. Because the living room has a window, and the window alone was as big as his whole civil service apartment. And so the detective saw Lake Zell, and really, all of Zell below him, I mean, splendid, you've got to admit.

And so he'd found his way back again. He couldn't quite see the Glockner Dam across the way, but right next to the Mooser Dam he saw something gleaming in the sun, and that was the funicular station at Heidnische Kirche.

"Have a seat!" Vergolder says.

But the living room, too, or, the living hall, let's call it, was completely stuffed full of antique furniture. And that's why Brenner didn't know all over again, where am I supposed to sit down.

Instead he went over to the window and turned his back to Vergolder, because he was looking out the window. Maybe just so that he wouldn't have to be constantly looking at the heap of antique furniture, which was really getting to feel oppressive. And while he's looking out the window, he says:

"What's with the bogus alibi that you gave the police—did you not want to protect yourself?"

"Do have a seat!" Vergolder says.

But Brenner didn't react, just kept looking out the

panoramic window—why the Historical Landmarks Pres-
ervation Commission allowed a window like that to get
installed in a place like this, please, don't even get me started.
He only turned around when the maid brought the tea in.
A slight, maybe sixteen-year-old girl that he'd seen in town
a few times. Now, as long as the maid was there, Vergolder
struck up a harmless tone.

"A tragic story, the death of my in-laws. But, you know
what I console myself with? They met while skiing. Nineteen twenty-nine, on a ski trip to Vermont. And they died
together in a ski lift. And then I think to myself: Maybe it
was supposed to be that way, just so I can find some consola-
tion in that."

Vergolder lit up a cigarette, and Brenner thought, Interesting, ever since I've gone off cigarettes, I've only had
to deal with people who are chain smokers. He waited for
Vergolder to say something about the accusation. But, as
soon as the girl left, he only put on his kids' coaching look
again and said:

"Why is it exactly that you're not on the force anymore?"

But not what you're thinking, that it was a question. No,
more like an answer is how it sounded. And needless to say,
it was, too. Because Vergolder knew for a fact why Brenner
wasn't on the force anymore. Just like Brenner already knew
the answer to his own question, I mean, why the false alibi.

In truth Brenner was preoccupied with a completely
different question now. This whole time he'd been asking
himself, What is it about the millionaire's tanned face that

bothers me so much. Not something strange but something familiar, maybe it was an imperceptible resemblance to his nephew Lorenz after all.

"Your alibi, the story about Lorenz. You didn't want us to fall for it in order to protect yourself, no, it was to protect Lorenz."

Vergolder had a peculiar look about him, like a person who's just taken their glasses off and can't see too much now. It seemed to Brenner like those nearsighted eyes of his didn't fit in somehow with his millionaire's face. Eyes, though, pure exaggeration. Just slits, that's what they were, if you tried to guess what color they were, not a chance.

And the whole time he was running his index finger over his eyelids in a way that would've made you think, dead tired. He had thousands of very fine wrinkles around his eyes, practically crow's feet, that's what it's called. Maybe you're familiar with how mountain climbers, as they get older, or old smokers, they don't mind this kind of upper-lip concertina. And so he was stroking his eyelids non-stop—you would've thought he was trying to iron out his concertina's folds.

"I had them operated on two months ago. A wonderful thing. Since then I don't need glasses anymore. But out on the slopes, just blinding, terrible."

"You've always known that Lorenz wrote the threat letters. Best wishes from the Heidnische Kirche," Brenner says.

"Don't get sore at me, Simon," Vergolder says. Because, you see, he was used to being able to call everybody by their first names. The Lift Kaiser of Zell, it'd been a long time since he'd asked, may I call you by your first name.

"It's no secret to anybody, what do you think you're revealing, Simon," Vergolder says, "everybody in Zell knew from the start. Only my Lorenz could come up with something like that."

"And you saw to it that it got swept under the rug," Brenner says.

"What rug?" Vergolder says. "What was I supposed to do? The tourists get nervous. What with the dam walls right over our heads."

"So, Lorenz had to back up his threat. With a few dead bodies in the ski lift," Brenner says.

"That's exactly how it would've been spun. By morons like you, Simon. Except that Lorenz is the absolute last person on this earth who'd kill another person. Sure, he hears the grass screaming when it's being mowed. But if he ever committed a murder, well, I'd volunteer to be the corpse!"

"Then he wouldn't have needed your false alibi at all. Which you came up with for him when he had to give an alibi for you. And you wouldn't have needed to pick him up in such a hurry from the psychiatric clinic, either, just so he wouldn't go and tell me anything different. And you wouldn't have needed to intercept the *Pinzgauer Post*, either, so that the newspaper would promptly forget the whole thing. If you were so convinced of his innocence."

Vergolder placed his half-empty teacup on the silver tray and poured himself a fresh cup. Then he gave Brenner's still-full cup a look of reproach. And then he looked at Brenner like maybe the kids' coach looks at the eight-year-old striker that he's trying to drum some courage into before a game and says:

"Why won't you sit down?"

"I prefer to stand," Brenner says.

"Are you afraid of sitting?" Vergolder says. "Are you afraid you'll have to move out of your civil service apartment?"

"You know all sorts of things about me," Brenner says.

"That you want to pin my in-laws' murder on me, for example. If Nemec hadn't been there. You probably would've put me in prison."

Needless to say, this was nonsense. Nemec was the one who'd wanted to dunk Vergolder. And it was Nemec, too, who gave Brenner the investigation orders at the time.

And just when it became clear that it wasn't going anywhere, Nemec nudged it over to Brenner. But it didn't matter to Brenner. That was just the last straw. When he said to himself, There's no point anymore, and then he chucked his badge at them. Although, I'll say it again and again, these days, when you're forty-four, well, hats off to a thing like that.

And all that about the civil service apartment. That had Brenner thinking all over again, Maybe there's a possibility that his classmate Schwaighofer could get him a one- or two-year deferral.

"You don't know about everything as much as I thought you did," Brenner says. "You don't even know that Lorenz doesn't even need an alibi from you because he's already got one! Lorenz thinks he has to lie for your sake."

"All the better," Vergolder says.

"Just tell the truth finally. It's all a huge misunderstanding. Lorenz believes he has to protect you and you believe you have to protect Lorenz."

"All the better for me and Lorenz," Vergolder says.

With that, though, he promptly rang for the maid. She saw the guest out, and Brenner lost all sense of where he was again because it was only a few steps to the front door, and before, he'd had to follow Vergolder up stairs and through hallways.

It seemed to him like in those pictures, maybe you know them, where the people are going up a staircase, up and up, but suddenly they're back where they started, so, what's there can't actually be real because—constantly going up and suddenly right back at the bottom. There's a painter who does that kind of thing, makes you real nervous. But it was actually calming Brenner down now since it meant he'd caught on to Vergolder's human weakness. That he was an antiques show-off and had schlepped Brenner through half his castle.

But the maid seemed to take notice that he didn't know where he was anymore, and she couldn't help but smile a little. Now, she had a painted incisor. A kind of neon color she had on it, on one of her incisors. Needless to say, Brenner recognized Clare Corrigan right away now.

Her name was actually Elfi Lohninger. Engljähringer told him that she'd dropped out of school. And that the people were talking about her being one of Vergolder's "*Nebenzu*," she told him that, too. But, the fact that Clare was now working as a maid at Vergolder's, well, she didn't tell him that.

Kati just gave him Elfi's composition book to take with him. But then Mandl showed up and sent Brenner off packing to Vergolder's. And now the book was just lying in his room at the Hirschenwirt, and he still hadn't gotten around to reading it yet.

CHAPTER 9

"6th Grade," it said on the book. "Clare Corrigan." But the name was crossed out, and in somebody else's handwriting it said: Lohninger, Elfriede. The last composition in the book was on the theme: The Significance of Our Reservoir as a National Symbol.

But you almost couldn't read the composition anymore, because it'd been marked up in red all over the place. And written at the end:

"Unsatisfactory!"

And now, this was the same handwriting that wrote "Lohninger, Elfriede" on the cover, namely, Engljähringer's handwriting.

"Completely off topic!" Engljähringer scrawled on, but for Brenner it was the complete opposite, for him, of course, the topic was spot-on:

"I'd like to write a little bit about a company that's played an important role in the building of the dam."

That's how she started off. And the very first word, Engljähringer the schoolteacher had scribbled under it in red—must've been because maybe you don't begin a composition with "I," like they used to say about letter-writing.

But Brenner was reminded of another scribbly red line now, the one that was the wrinkle in Mandl's furrowed forehead when he found Brenner on Engljähringer's couch.

"The company was an American chemical company. It provided the Austrian companies with the necessary know-how for them to manufacture high-grade concrete for the three dam walls."

Engljähringer the schoolteacher had put the American know-how in brackets and written the more domestic *Fachwissen* above it.

> "I would like to write about what this company did beforehand in America. Maybe I should write about why I know about it. My father married the boss's daughter. I'm not from this marriage, though, I'm a secret. This is why secrets have always interested me more than the official story, because I myself am a secret. So, I would prefer to write about what I know about the company, because the dam, well, what's there to say about it except for it produces electricity."

"Far too long of an introduction!!!" Engljähringer the schoolteacher wrote in the margin of this paragraph. And everywhere else, too—the page was just teeming with red marks. Brenner refused to believe that this was one and the same hand now. That the hand of Engljähringer, translucent freckles crawling all the way up to the fingernails, had caused this massacre. And even thundering out three exclamation marks with that red pen of hers.

"My father married the daughter of the boss of this American chemical company. I don't think it had anything to do with the fact that my father was a gilder and the company in America manufactured glow-in-the-dark watch faces. But it fits somehow, gold and glow-in-the-dark paint, I think, the one shines by day, the other by night. And the boss's father, he was the founder of the company. His name was Parson, and the company was called Parson Radium, and the luminous paint that made him extremely rich, was called "Light Night.""

"Why so wordy?" the red pen of Engljähringer the schoolteacher asked, but Brenner wasn't letting it distract him anymore now.

"Soon, old man Parson had two hundred dial painters working for him. This was around 1915. Above all, young women. They had to lick their brushes so that they could shape them into a fine enough tip to paint the tiny watch numerals. Sometimes the painters would paint their fingernails or teeth just for fun because, then, they would light up in the dark, too. Unfortunately, one after another, they died. So, there was an investigation."

This was now the point where the phone rang in Brenner's hotel room, it must've been around two in the afternoon. But he didn't get it. But then it wouldn't quit ringing, so then he did go get it.

"Brenner here."

At that exact moment, though, the caller hung up.

"Son of a …" Brenner grumbled, then sat back down again with the composition book.

He couldn't find his place again right away, and so he picked it up a little too far down. And so, he read that the results of the investigation were kept a secret. He didn't know what all that about the results was about, though, because that was in the paragraph that he'd skipped over. Needless to say, now he's curious and backs up to read:

"So, there was an investigation. The investigation was secret. The doctors observed the workers in a dark room. There, the hair, faces, arms, necks, clothes, and undergarments of the dial painters glowed in the dark. Even the dial painters' breath glowed in the dark."

Now Brenner was back where he was before. It struck him that, there on the second page, there were almost no red marks anymore.

Needless to say, two possibilities. Either Engljähringer had become exactly as enthralled by the story as he himself was now and completely forgot about marking it while she read. Or, it was already clear by this point that there was nothing but an F in it for Clare, and Engljähringer thought, Off-topic, and why should I bother correcting one page more?

"Parson kept the results of the investigation secret. The work conditions for the painters remained the same for years. Until there got to be so many victims that Parson had to appear in court. But he was found not guilty. Thanks to the victims being in apparent good health. That is, at the onset of contamination the victims felt better than usual. This was because the body produces an especially large number of blood cells as resistance. Red probably. And then, suddenly it stops doing that. That's why the epidemic went unnoticed for years. But according to the law, any lawsuits seeking reparations must be brought within two years, at the latest, from the onset of the illness. And the epidemic was triggered by "Light Night" much earlier than that. For example, on November 16, 1922, one of the painters was on her way to work at the glow-in-the-dark factory. She felt perfectly healthy. Her bones were so brittle, though, that her leg broke while she walked. One week later, she died. She was twenty-seven years old. Her name was Clare Corrigan."

Now, though. The teacher had finally given up on correcting. The last two pages, she just, pfffffffffffffffft, got it? Top to bottom, I'm talking diagonal, crossed out. Those were the pages where Clare described how the company's history carried on.

First, Parson developed a non-hazardous glow-in-the-dark type of manufacturing, then, WWII, so he sold the glow-in-the-dark fittings to the Americans for their planes. Needless to say, that was a huge deal, because nobody else could have delivered that. Millions, boy, I don't need to tell you.

And after the war, immediately switched saddles to erector chemistry, in other words, construction materials. Because they were thinking, after the war, people are building, and so they specialized in high-grade concrete mixtures.

Brenner, now: Aha! effect. Because what do you need for a dam, high-grade concrete, of course, and where do the Zellers get their high-grade concrete from right after the war. Now, the Zellers got a bit of a leg up there from the Americans. That was still Parson junior, though, who got that all set up. Not too far from the place where just fifty years later he'd be found on a ski lift.

Brenner had to read her scribbling a few more times before, little by little, he could make sense of it. And he needed the most time for the last few sentences. Because Clare had literally filled her composition book, I mean, full up to the last page. And then she still wasn't done. She wrote the conclusion on the inside of the back cover. The cover was blue, though, so it was blue written on blue now.

"Parson expanded to Europe. And to Zell, a huge contract, where during the war hundreds of prisoners of war built (DIED) the dam. And now the Americans sent their own prisoners of war (US) up there, dying by the dozens, too. And 1951, the Symbol of the Republic, finally complete."

Brenner stared out at the lake a few minutes, but then— all of the sudden the room felt too small to him. Put his shoes on and wanted to walk down to the lake. But once he set foot on the street, he went the opposite direction. Not down to the lake but up to Dreifaltigkeitsgasse. And, goes without saying, at the end of Dreifaltigkeitsgasse was the Feinschmeck Café.

Interesting, though. Someone must've run electricity through the Feinschmeck's door handle just for kicks. Alright, don't get me wrong now. Brenner had the door to the Feinschmeck open just a crack—immediately sees Nemec sitting there. Needless to say, electroshock. Shut the door immediately, of course. But, interesting! From the shock, he lost control of his muscles. Needed a few seconds before the glass door, which weighed a ton, would finally shut.

Maybe, though, this was only on account of the hydraulic door-closer that was there to keep the door from slamming. That must've been it. This is what Brenner was preoccupied with as he walked back down Dreifaltigkeitsgasse. Because he didn't want to think about what kind of business Nemec suddenly had back in Zell. And he didn't want to know why Nemec had called him earlier. Because suddenly Brenner was quite certain now that it could only have been Nemec. Who else would let the phone ring till it won't ring anymore.

But he couldn't think about the hydraulic door-closer and the telephone ringing forever. Another distraction's needed now. Brenner buys himself the *Pinzgauer Post* and takes it down to the lake. But instead of reading the paper, he does something completely different. Because when you've had a shock, you're often capable of things in the moment that you normally wouldn't be. Like a bolt of lightning now, Brenner makes a decision, and he makes his way to Perterer Jr.'s for the Walther.

But one thing you can't forget. Brenner was still a ditherer, through and through.

He had another reason for not deciding on a gun for

months now. Perterer Sr. shot himself not quite two months before the lift scandal. So every time Brenner was in the gun shop, he thought: Maybe it wouldn't hurt any if I get to talking one more time with Perterer Jr. a little.

"The Walther it is," Perterer Jr. said with a smile. But you could tell he hadn't been a salesman very long. Because now that Brenner's finally come to a decision, Perterer Jr. says:

"Although. The Glock has its advantages, too, of course."

"The Glock, yes, and to think, it was almost the Glock."

"All synthetic. No rust, no mess, no nothing. And if you throw it in the water, it still works."

"Or in the snow."

"The American police sure know why they've got the Glock."

"The police don't know everything."

"No, especially ours," Perterer Jr. said, laughing, because he was the kind of guy, if something amused him—instantly laughed his head off. But, then, kept right on talking in all seriousness:

"One thing I'd be interested in. In a case like this, what did the police do exactly with their binoculars?"

Now, in twenty years on the force, Brenner had never had binoculars. A gun, always, but never binoculars. For a moment he thought Perterer Jr. was just such an inexperienced salesman that he thought he could possibly peddle binoculars to the police. Because it's not just pistols and rifles in a gun shop. They've also got scopes and perfectly ordinary field glasses on display at Perterer's.

"Maybe the border patrol, maybe they've got binoculars

there. But I don't think you could sell them on binoculars very easy. Because the police—you'd grow old trying in a bureaucracy like that."

"Now I've gone and said the wrong thing," Perterer Jr. says, because this was a polite young man, they taught him in the way of manners in Paris, he never would've said: No, you've misunderstood me.

"I mean, the Americans' binoculars. What the police did with them, if they found the binoculars when they found the murder victims. Because they were brand new."

Needless to say, Brenner had completely forgot by now that the Americans had binoculars with them on the lift. They weren't regular binoculars, though, more like your finer opera glasses. And that's the kind of thing a tourist is bound to keep on him.

"Did you sell them the binoculars?"

"The American came in here himself."

"I don't know, either, then, what the police did with the binoculars exactly. Probably went to the next of kin. On the other hand, evidence. Might still be with the police."

"Pity, because they were still brand new. 'A surprise for my wife,' the American said, when he came in to pick the binoculars up. But, to be honest, if I were a millionaire today, I would've have come up with a better gift for my sixtieth wedding anniversary."

"And he came in here himself and bought them."

"He ordered them from my father. Then, picked them up from me. Maybe a week before Alois found them on the lift. Because it took months for the glasses to arrive from

America. Special order, of course. He knew exactly what he wanted, the old American."

"Unlike me," Brenner says, and explains to Perterer Jr. that he's going to have to think it all over again, the Walther. Because he's thinking, Maybe it wouldn't hurt if I talked with Perterer Jr. just one more time.

Then, Brenner walked halfway around the lake. But it wasn't until he was tired, sitting on a bench and looking out at Zell that he truly noticed it. The promenade along the lake was completely empty of people. When there aren't people here, it's so nice here, suddenly you realize why everybody wants to be here, he thought. Then he picked up the *Pinzgauer Post* and on the first page:

"Resurrection of the Dead!"

Mandl must've been the scribe behind that piece of poetry. Easter was still months off, and besides: directly beneath the headline was a photo of the American lift passengers.

And beneath the photo it said that several of the Parsons' checks had been signed, dated, and cashed. Over a hundred thousand schillings the Parsons had withdrawn from their account. And, this, half a year after their deaths.

CHAPTER 10

Now, you should know, a professional fire department you're only apt to find in the big cities. Everywhere else, a volunteer fire department, because, the young men go and volunteer, the fire department does a festival, a ball, let's say, and things just aren't on fire all that much in the country.

More likely's a car accident, you know, Saturday night, gotta cut somebody out. Because, for the young people, a car's important out in the country, there's a disco, it's in the next town over, now you're going to need a car, of course.

Then, it gets to be two in the morning, or even three, four, too. Alcohol now, and then they drive home, everybody having a good time, girls, too, in the car—of course, now you've got to cut them out, too, more often than not.

But a fire, per se, rarely ever. Maybe a farm, if the hay's not completely dry and a farmer puts damp hay on a fire, needless to say, burns the whole farm down.

Rare, though. Some young buck could be in the fire department a long time, let's say, already worn his Class A's to two fireman's balls, but never been in a fire. Already cut ten people out, or a retiree locks herself out of her apartment, stuff like that, or for my part, a kitchen fire, but he gives it a quick spritz and it's out.

Now, unfortunately. It happens time and again that one of these young firemen who's never been in a fire before gets ideas. Poor devil lights something on fire just so he can put it out. We've all done it. Weissbach once, one time at Bruck, and Eschenau, I know, once before.

But this has nothing to do with our story, with the Americans in the lift. No, just so you understand why it was Alois the Lift that night, the fourteenth of September, why he's so alarmed now. Even though he'd been fire chief ten years already, more than ten years, because he got the medal last summer. But in Zell there hadn't been a fire in almost three years.

And now, at a gas station of all places. Twelve minutes to ten the siren goes off, fourteenth of September, it was a Thursday, Alois the Lift already in his pajamas.

Into the parka he goes now, and there he's sitting in his Renault Twingo, nothing but pajamas and a parka on, but no matter, he's going to have to slip into his uniform anyway.

Two minutes later he's already down at the firehouse, three, four others already there ahead of him, gas station's on fire now, and the firemen are racing from all over, four minutes later they're all there, five minutes the first truck's off.

Needless to say, if the captain's nervous, the whole squad gets infected. Seidl was the driver, fifteen years he'd been the driver for the fire department, a driver elsewise, too, professionally, I mean, chauffeur to Frächter Hasenauer. Took the first curve right out of the gate too fast. You'd like to think he knows it like the back of his hand and has driven it a thousand times in the fire truck, and every time as fast as it'll go, but this time: too fast.

Not that anything happened, nothing happened at all, had to put it in reverse is all, power steering, no problem, and loses maybe ten seconds that he makes right back up again. Only—the nervousness was there. No wonder, because, a gas station, needless to say, this was the first time, first time for everybody, not just the boys, but for everybody, for the chief, too.

And then the training video. It was in France some—I don't know, fifty or sixty years ago. The old guys had all seen it a few times already, and the young guys, at least once, because just this past July—so, just a couple months ago—Alois the Lift played the old training video for them again. Because there was a gas station in Cannes that caught fire, and so you could see exactly what the French firefighters did wrong.

Needless to say, what the Zell firemen had to be thinking right about now, how in Cannes, their colleagues as it were, how they all got blown to pieces together. Because nobody came out of it. That much you could see on the video, real nice, that's why it was always used for training purposes, because you could see exactly what the French firefighters did wrong.

Goes without saying, though. Not much you need to do wrong, and you're already in the air. And naturally that's what was going through the heads of the Zell firemen now on the drive over there. Because the French, just a few meters too close, and you'd have thought: atomic bomb.

And so you noticed it right away, every single one of the firemen was more nervous than usual, not just the young ones, but the old guys, every bit as nervous. Because everything's got to move awfully fast, of course, and it's only on the drive over that they're getting their uniforms in order, I'm talking buttoning-up, lacing up their boots, helmet, gloves. It's in the details that you'd notice it now—if his laces aren't tight, or let's say, misses a button, he's nervous.

Three minutes later Seidl's already up at the furniture store. Drove so fast he made up those ten seconds twice over. At least. Because behind the furniture store is the Aral gas station. And as he pulls in behind the furniture store, a couple of the young firemen jump clear off. Before they'd been sitting completely stiff, and all of the sudden, they're leaping up, and Niederwieser even let out a cry.

Because the gas station wasn't on fire at all. Now, how does a thing like this happen, that an experienced fire chief like Alois the Lift mixes up the gas stations. And to make matters worse, the Shell station's all the way over on the other side of Zell. But, you could see it all the way across the lake, even from here, from the Aral station, you could see that the Shell station was on fire over there, because the flames were reflected by half the lake.

But this only happened to Alois the Lift, because, thirty years he'd been gassing up and always at the Aral station, because he bought his first car in sixty-six, an old Beetle, and at the time, there was only Aral. So he commands Seidl to the

Aral gas station, autopilot, even though he'd understood for a fact "Shell station" when the fire got reported.

At that moment, where he sees the Aral gas station there in front of him and it's not on fire, it hits him immediately, of course. Besides, you only had to glance over. The Shell station was on fire. Or better put, the way it looked, you'd have thought the entire north exit was in flames. Because when a gas station like that's on fire, well, I don't need to tell you.

"Correction to the address of the fire! Shell gas station, north exit!" Alois the Lift barked into his walkie-talkie. Because there were two more fire trucks following after them, and they needed to know, too. Needless to say, though, all his barking was useless. You can't get from the Aral gas station to the Shell gas station in under five minutes, doesn't matter if Seidl's driving or somebody else.

When they finally got there, everybody else was already there, of course: police, ambulance, newspaper, all there. Only thing not there, fire department.

As Alois the Lift leaps out of the truck, he lands right at the feet of Postmaster Kollarik. And Kollarik, there's an irascible dog for you, the Zellers always call him "Choleric," only when he wasn't around, of course. And he's shouting at Alois the Lift now, stroke of luck that Alois doesn't understand him. Because when a gas station like this is really burning, the noise, of course, enough to make you think: Judgment Day.

But Alois the Lift doesn't even see Postmaster Kollarik now. People would later say that Alois the Lift led like a commando, not nervous one bit, like a robot, and so hyper-calm, like on TV when you see a UN general. Walkie-talkie and totally calm, people would say time and again.

Now, can the fire department really do anything at all when a gas station like this is on fire. True, insofar as the gas station itself goes, you can forget it. An extinguishing agent, of course, foam, but that burns out, just hopeless. The surrounding area, though, all the more important. Start by securing the fire. Because the onlookers, needless to say, there's more deaths for you than from the fire itself if you don't secure everything right away. You've really got to crack down, because, people, if there's something to look at, they'll go running right into that burning gas station.

Now, the *gendarmerie* took a hard look at the clock when the fire department didn't show up right away, but when it comes to securing the fire, never heard of it. Those people were standing way too close, and if something had exploded, there wouldn't have been a single ambulance for them, because, the ambulances, also parked way too close. So Alois the Lift dives right in, so fast he kicks up a cloud of soot. Two minutes later everybody's standing 250 meters back.

Meanwhile the team's schlepped the pump down to the lake. No fire lane there, no, on account of the train tracks in between and a narrow pedestrian underpass that's too tight for the pump. So they have to schlep the pump over the train tracks.

After, they tear down the fencing. Because there's wire fencing a meter high between the street and the tracks, just like there is between the tracks and the lake. You couldn't have looked fast enough, fire department already had that fencing torn down. Then, guided the hoses right over the tracks, because nobody could bring a train through anyway. Imagine, gas station explodes—that whole train would've blew right with it.

That's always the big question when a gas station's on fire. As a fireman, you've always got this feeling right there in the crook of your neck. Is it going to blow up, or is it not going to blow up. Objective one: secure the fire. Objective two: secure the adjacent structures. Objective three: now, will it blow up, or will it not blow up.

Later, on the video, you could see quite clearly how Alois the Lift took command. So calm, nobody ever would've got the idea that it was his first gas station. Because one of the firemen always has to be there with a video camera, used to be a camera-camera, on account of the insurance and that kind of thing, you've just got to do it, but these days, only video anymore, and for that they've got two people that get trained extra. And so you could clearly see how, first, Alois secured the fire, all the onlookers 250 meters back, no one allowed down at the lake, either, because the shore's way too close. And, then, immediately secured the neighboring buildings.

First, evacuate the people, second, secure the buildings. But you can't just spritz the buildings down with water so that they don't start burning, too, because the building, maybe water damage—just as expensive as if it'd just burned down.

But, at least the bordering buildings weren't apartment buildings. No, warehouse and Lengauer's used Mercedes dealership. And the warehouse roof truss was already glowing a bit on the one side, now, so of course you've got to spritz. Water damage or no water damage, you can't let the whole warehouse burn down.

Needless to say, all of this in a matter of seconds. Warehouse cleared out so that the water doesn't ruin the whole harvest. September's, no less. And all the while: Is it going to blow or is it not going to blow. Because a gas station like this has got tanks underground. Even though it's all so well-secured that you might ask yourself how it could catch fire at all. Once it's burning, though, all the more dangerous.

You simply don't know what's going on underground with the tanks. Are they burning already or are they not burning already, you can't exactly look under the ground. Now, as long as they're only burning, it's not so bad. But, exploding, of course, that's what the gasses are doing. At a certain temperature. Which is why you've got to spray down the asphalt above the tanks the whole time, cooling it, I mean, so that the tanks don't reach that temperature.

Because, as long as the temperature stays low enough, it burns and burns but doesn't blow. So, cooling on the one hand, but on the other, not getting too close, because you see it all too well on the video, in Cannes, or wherever that was. The fire department was cooling the tanks, but they were already so hot that they exploded anyway, and then the firefighters were standing too close, and then, needless to say, good night.

It bears mention, though, how Alois the Lift took command: hats off. Now, you should know, the fire chief gets selected—it's no job, no, you're chosen. An assembly, and that's where the members of the volunteer fire department select their chief. On account of the statutes, of course. And Alois the Lift had been fire chief for over ten years—there's no two ways about it, anybody else, out of the question. But how he'd mixed up the gas stations, at first he thought: all over now. You've had a good run as fire chief.

The prospect was so depressing to Alois, though, that all fear fell away from him all at once. After nearly eleven years, that everything should suddenly be over and done with on account of five minutes. Fire chief no more, that seemed worse to him than what'd happened to his colleagues in Cannes.

Interesting, though, that's just how people are. Of all the reasons for him to be this calm and not to make any mistakes. Because, at that moment, he almost would've preferred it if they'd all got blown up. A good thing these people don't know.

And today, throughout Europe, they use the Zell video in their fire department trainings. You can clearly see on it how Alois whistled back the fire brigade that had been cooling the tanks underground. Because there stood eight men, two to a hose, and doing nothing but spraying at where the tanks were, beneath the asphalt. You have to do it in any event, even if you're hoping, of course, that nothing in the tanks is burning.

But one thing you don't see on the training video, and that's what Alois the Lift saw now. Because when the surface of the asphalt turns soft and runny, you don't see that so easy at night, even if the fire's got it all lit up just fine. The asphalt wasn't exactly running off in streams, no—only if you looked very close would you've seen that it'd turned runny and soft.

And when Alois the Lift saw that now, that all the sudden the asphalt was turning soft there, he knew, of course, that it must be pretty warm below. The rest, well, you can see just as easy on the video.

How Alois called back his men. And then, you see how at first they only took a few steps back. And then, you see how Alois straight-out tore them back with his own hands. And then, two seconds later, at most, you see—you've got to picture it like how those war planes, how they can blast off vertically. That's how the whole gas station slowly lifted into the air—vertically.

Needless to say, Alois the Lift realized now that the eight he'd called back would select him again, guaranteed, as their chief.

CHAPTER 11

The Zell cemetery is only about 200 meters from the Shell gas station. To walk from the post office to the Hirschenwirt, it's farther. Maybe it's even only 150 meters between the gas station and the cemetery wall. But those few meters make all the difference.

The gas station, of course, is right on the way into town. Or better put, it was. And it was right where the gas station was that it started to feel like Zell. Even though the sign for Zell is posted half a kilometer before. Somehow, though, it's a matter of feeling.

Now, the cemetery's only a few steps beyond the gas station, also way after the sign on the road, well, in the vicinity, speed limit fifty, but anyway, believe it or not. The cemetery more or less borders the gas station, and nevertheless, the gas station feels like it's inside city limits and the cemetery feels clearly outside.

No Zeller is going to tell you the cemetery is inside city limits because every one of them's got the feeling that, when he goes to the cemetery, he's leaving Zell. And even though it's only those couple of meters, nobody walks to the cemetery, no, practically everybody drives because you've got the feeling like you're leaving Zell.

If you just need something from the gas station real quick, maybe a fuse, you'd walk, but if you're going to the cemetery, maybe if you've got an anniversary of somebody's death, light a candle, let's say, flowers, then you drive, guaranteed.

So you can only imagine what the parking lot looked like when they buried Vergolder. All parked up, side of the road, up till the gas station, and even at the gas station itself, a few people parked among the rubble. Because it wasn't hot anymore, just reeked still, but you smelled it all over Zell anyway. This was on a Wednesday, exactly one week after the explosion.

Now, pay attention, the gas station blew up on the fourteenth, so now: the twenty-first of September. And still, the summer heat, nobody could remember it having ever been like this. Indian summer, sure, but not non-stop like this since I don't know when. Practically climate change. A lot of folks didn't know, what should I wear to the funeral now, because way too warm for the black coat, and these days not everybody's got a black coat or a black dress. And, needless to say, all of Zell came out for Vergolder, for his funeral.

And now, the next day, this was Thursday, they buried Lorenz. Because it occurred to the priest that the victim and the murderer, I mean, how's that going to look if they're buried together. But "bury" isn't completely accurate, of course. Because these days when you're burned alive at a gas station, needless to say, not much left over for you to bury, per se. At this point, it was more of a symbolic business, but a proper funeral, nevertheless.

Now, when they buried Lorenz on Thursday, you'd like to think much less people are apt to go. Interesting, though. They all came back on Thursday, and believe it or not, all drove again, too, of course—World Cup, you'd have thought.

Only Brenner damn well walked, of course. But, then, he had to stand all penned in just like everybody else at the cemetery.

"The flowers on Vergolder's grave still look quite fresh," from behind him, a woman's voice whispered directly into his left ear.

"Even though they've been out here twenty-six hours," another woman's voice whispered into his right ear.

This amused Brenner, how precisely they'd calculated, because they'd buried Vergolder at one and Lorenz at three, so, twenty-six hours, they were exactly right.

"That's fall for you," the woman standing behind his left ear whispered again now. And even though she was whispering and you can't recognize a voice very easy that way, Brenner realized that he knew this voice from somewhere.

"Where do you see any sign of fall?" the other voice whispered in his other ear.

"One hell of a fall, then, twenty-nine degrees, hotter than it was all summer."

"Hot, yes, but the fall air," whispered the left voice, but he still couldn't think of where he knew it from. And whispered from the right now:

"The lake air does that. Fresh breeze constantly blowing off the lake, you know how good that is for the flowers."

"Lake air, we've got that all year long."

Who does this voice belong to? Brenner wondered, and it was starting to needle him that he couldn't place it. When he tried to turn around, though, he didn't get too far. Because he immediately found himself looking at the German. She wasn't standing behind him, though. He only had to turn his head a few centimeters, and there he was, looking at the German, all the way over on the other side.

Needless to say, Brenner immediately forgot about the two women behind him now. Because needless to say, Handless wasn't alone. She had Andi with her, well, on her—he was more or less hanging onto her arm. The arms on her were perfectly normal, healthy, I mean, just at the bottom of them, no hands. And then there's Andi, just—hanging, you've almost got to call it. If you took the German away, you'd have thought he'd fall straight into Lorenz's grave. Because the pair of them were standing right up front, sideways next to the priest, on the long side of the grave, so to speak.

And it was exactly the same as yesterday now. Yesterday, too, Brenner had observed how Andi hung onto the German so tight that you'd have thought Andi wasn't going to make it much longer himself, and then there'd be a third funeral. Even though the disaster had left him completely unscathed, and about that, you've got to say: as if by some miracle.

Because Andi was just sitting there in the Shell shop when Vergolder pulled in to gas up. Lorenz was back at the gas station with Andi, keeping him company like he did almost every day. And then, just as his uncle drives up in his four-by-four, Lorenz goes out. This was all in the *Pinzgauer Post*.

And all week long, nothing else was getting talked about in Zell, of course. Nice and slow it was sinking in. And somebody always knows a little more than the next guy. Brenner had to tune in everywhere, and it seemed like his ears were hurting him now. Because, needless to say, a lot of nonsense you've got to listen to.

But yesterday at the Vergolder funeral, the German told him something completely different. "Something completely different" is right because she actually told him something that doesn't necessarily belong at a funeral. You're going to laugh, though; it happens more often than you'd care to believe that people at a funeral start telling jokes.

As his gaze brushed over the German, Brenner tried to remember the joke she'd whispered to him yesterday in the middle of the funeral. But, nothing doing, the joke was gone. And the German herself seemed like a different person to him today. For a second he couldn't tell, was Andi hanging onto the German or was she hanging onto him, and it seemed to him almost like she was crying, although, well, naturally. He was way too far away from her to be able to say.

Now something else occurred to Brenner, though. But not the joke that the German had told him yesterday in the middle of the funeral, because remembering jokes had never come easy to Brenner. He was all the more surprised, then, that the joke he'd heard years ago at the funeral for his colleague Schmeller should occur to him now. Because he got shot during a bank robbery, and as they were lowering his coffin, Haslauer started in on this joke.

So you see, Lorenz's funeral was more upsetting to Brenner than he would've had himself believe. Because psychology, of course. And these days when you start telling jokes at a funeral, then it's perfectly obvious. Brenner had gotten to know Lorenz, and somehow he became, I don't want to say, well, sympathetic. But Brenner did take himself by surprise when he remembered that he was actually the one who'd told the joke.

Lorenz, that nut, blew himself up, practically suicide commando. Vergolder drives into the gas station, and Lorenz says to Andi, I'll take care of it, and Andi doesn't think anything of it, because Lorenz often helped him out. And besides, he was glad not to have anything to do with Vergolder. First of all, no tip, and second of all, their ongoing battle over the cigarettes, because Vergolder was always standing around the gas station with a lit cigarette.

So, Lorenz goes out, okay, grabs the nozzle, and you've got picture it like this, like when two children are squirting each other with the garden hose. Lorenz, from two meters away, aims directly for his uncle's face with the gasoline. And then there's the lit cigarette, too. Then, needless to say. A second later the two are standing in flames and so is the whole gas station.

A miracle that Andi walked away from it, well, he ran for his life, because—impossible he could've done anything to help.

Now Brenner's standing there at the funeral and all the sudden he remembers that he feels sorry for Lorenz. Not normal pity, let's say, the way you do for every human being, but more than for, say, Vergolder.

And now that Lorenz had killed his uncle's American mother and father-in-law. Brenner himself was surprised, it just didn't seem right to him. But it was in the *Pinzgauer Post*. Right next to a photo of Nemec. CASE CLOSED, it said right under Nemec's picture. Awkward for Brenner now, of course, he starts sympathizing with Lorenz all the sudden.

And next to the photo of Nemec is one of Andi. Eyewitness report. Mandl interviewed Andi while he was still in the hospital, and maybe that's the reason why Brenner hadn't talked with Andi at all. Because maybe he didn't want to be such a vulture like Mandl. And that's why he was content for the time being with what the people were saying. And with the report in the *Pinzgauer Post*. Even if Mandl's name was printed above it.

Just to be on the safe side, they immediately took Andi to the hospital on the night of the fire, that is, after they caught him down by the promenade on the lake. Because he was in a state of shock, of course, so much so that he'd run around half the lake. And then he resisted, shouting that he was uninjured. But, then, that, too, turned out to be true. And over at the hospital Mandl was waiting for him. He's always going sailing with the assistant medical director, so, needless to say, he got his interview just like that.

Naturally, Andi told Mandl that Vergolder alone was the guilty party:

"Vergolder always opened his gas cap himself, even though we're no self-service gas station."

And a thousand times Andi had pointed it out to him. That he should kindly not open his gas cap with a lit cigarette in his mouth.

"Lorenz hung out a lot at the gas station with me. Most of the time he just sat there and smoked. In the shop you can smoke. Sometimes he'd help me out, too. But I was surprised when his uncle came in to gas up that he went out to help him of all people. He can't stand his uncle. Me neither, of course. Got out of his four-by-four with a cigarette in his mouth just like he always did, of course. Lorenz says to me, Stay put, I'll take care of him."

Didn't matter how long Brenner thought about it, still nothing stuck out to him that would've made him say: inconsistency.

Now, though, all the sudden he notices that Nemec's standing next to him at the cemetery. And they're all packed in, of course, tight as sardines. Nemec's standing closer to Brenner now than he ever did all his years on the force, you might even say: physical contact.

So that he wouldn't inadvertently look to his left and at Nemec, Brenner jerks his head stiffly to the other side now, where Andi was clinging to the handless German's arm. But no matter how long he looked at Andi, or how often Andi's testimony from the *Pinzgauer Post* shot through his head, there was nothing that could've helped Brenner:

"I just sat there, surprised that Lorenz would go out to help his uncle. He took the nozzle out, but instead of sticking it in the tank of the four-by-four, he pointed it like a pistol at his uncle. Who's really the guilty one here because he had that cigarette burning in his mouth again. Of course he's standing in flames. And then, all I know is how the fire caught Lorenz and then the four-by-four, and then I see myself as I'm running on the promenade by the lake. There are a few hundred meters in between, but I don't know anymore, and then I hear the sirens and then the hospital."

"It used to be that everybody only put geraniums on the balcony, because they wintered well," Brenner hears that familiar voice now in his left ear.

"Geraniums, that's right. Not as pretty nowadays. Petunias though."

"Mm, very pretty, petunias. Very, very pretty. But tough to winter."

"Wintering, who even does that today. Since we got the sauna, I don't have any more room in the basement for wintering the balcony flowers."

"Well, you need a good place. And even then, with petunias, it's still not a sure thing."

Now, Brenner knew for a fact that he knew this voice. Knew it well. But he simply couldn't come up with who it belonged to. It was needling him so bad now that this little slip kept happening to him where he wants to turn around, but on the wrong side. And needless to say, he wasn't going to get very far with Nemec standing there. He looked Nemec right in the eyes. And Nemec grins at him and says:

"Do you know this one?"

It looked to Brenner like Nemec was nodding his head

in the priest's direction, who was just sprinkling those standing around him with holy water. Of course he knew the priest, it wasn't that long ago that he'd gave him the idea about Engljähringer. But the nimble little man from the Saturday-afternoon mass, it was like, transformed. With his pale, skeletal figure and his lopsided ash-blond head, he looked like he was laying it on a little thick for the funeral today. Now, a person's apt to ask himself, how does he pull a wedding off, or something cheerful, say, what does he do at a resurrection.

But, once again, Brenner had misunderstood his ex-boss's question. Because Nemec hadn't actually been nodding his head over at the priest. Really, Brenner had to have known what Nemec meant when he asked:

"Do you know this one?"

Because this was a habit of Nemec's. He always tossed his head back so peculiarly before he told a joke that you'd have thought he must be rattling a forgotten joke out of his subconscious and back into his memory again.

"Woman goes into a sex shop and buys a vibrator," Nemec says.

But Brenner turned his head demonstrably away and looked back at the priest.

"Asks the salesman how you use it, and he says, just like you would a man's penis."

Nemec wasn't even making an effort to whisper. An altar girl—that's the daughter of Fürstauer from over at the deli—passed the priest the censer now. And with solemn movements the priest wafted the smoke over the whole cemetery.

You'd have thought a gas station was burning somewhere.

You've got to picture it like this: he's holding the silver censer by the silver chain, high above his head, and that's how he swings it. And every time the censer swings back, it clinks against the silver chain: "clink—clink—clink—clink," you could hear it throughout the cemetery, even if you were standing in the back and couldn't see anything.

But Brenner saw it all of course. It didn't do him any good, either, I mean, that he was making a point of watching the priest as Nemec was trying to tell him his joke. Nemec showed no sign of irritation at all and said:

"Next day the woman goes back to the sex shop and wants to file a complaint."

The other altar girl passed the priest a little shovel that he strewed some dirt over Lorenz's grave with. And around the cemetery a few people started blowing their noses as the priest put on his doleful voice and said:

"Remember, O mortal, for dust you are and to dust you shall return."

Brenner didn't laugh at Nemec's joke, though. He didn't grimace. He just said:

"And so it was Lorenz who put the two Americans in the lift. All the sudden you guys are completely sure about that."

"Compweetwee pfshure!" the cop answered, still making like the toothless mouth of the woman in the sex shop. It only looked like he had no teeth, you know, with his lips sucked in over them like this. Nemec had always had such thin lips.

For a moment now, Brenner considered whether he should do what he'd surely been wanting to do a couple hundred times over these last few years. But, then, he didn't deck Nemec in the middle of the funeral. Instead, he said, while still not looking the toothless woman in the face:

"That's awfully convenient for you, anyway."

Now, not what you're thinking, that Brenner was actually doubting, let's say, that Lorenz had done it. It was more because, up against Nemec, nothing else occurred to him at that moment. Because it was in the *Pinzgauer Post* after all, and people weren't talking about anything else. That Lorenz had been sending these letters for years. Heidnische Kirche, that really only could've been Lorenz's idea. And then, of course: that Lorenz didn't get his savings passbook from Vergolder this year at Christmas.

And then, of course, the checks. Lorenz had a talent for drawing, Vergolder could've kept it hidden. Ran in the family. Just like everybody in the Moser family are all musical, or Mayr the butcher, they always make the best *Leberkäse*. Lorenz copied the signature, so exact it made the experts' eyes pop out of their sockets. But now that his photo had appeared in the paper, a bank teller remembered him.

"All that about the letters you guys figured out pretty fast, though," Brenner cut a little deeper.

"Actually, it should've been clear six months ago," Nemec says, "but, unfortunately, if you want something done right, you've got to do it yourself."

Now, of course. Six months ago, that was Brenner's job back then. He no longer had any desire to prove anything to

Nemec. Because Nemec had been the one who'd held him back at the time.

Brenner just wanted out of the cemetery now. But as he turned around, he was reminded all over again that the cemetery was stuffed full of mourners. Making it to the exit would be hopeless.

And besides. What good would it have done him if he'd gotten out of the cemetery. He wouldn't have known where to go. Because, before he turned around, he was still thinking he could go to the Feinschmeck. That he could go crawling back to Erni the waitress.

But Erni was right there with him. Serious and silent as a stuffed dress form, she stared at Brenner as he turned around. And she had such a look of despair that you'd have thought, she simply couldn't get over it—over Lorenz, his death, or over the question of how the flowers on her balcony would get through the winter.

CHAPTER 12

It goes without saying. There wasn't much else for Brenner to do in Zell now. For over half a year he'd lived in room 214 at the Hirschenwirt. But now he just wanted to write his report and just get on with it and out of Zell.

He understood now, too, why he'd been resisting the report so much this whole time. There must've been something in the air somehow that this would be his last report for the Meierling Detective Agency, the conclusion, so to speak.

What he didn't understand was why he was sitting all depressed in his room. Since he'd got back from the funeral at four-thirty, he'd been sitting on the edge of the bed, you'd have thought he'd been struck dumb right at the moment he was about to lie down. And he'd been studying the carpet pattern ever since, and, how should I put it, it was not a very interesting pattern.

Now one thing you can't forget. Brenner was the kind of person—how should I explain it to you. The job in Zell had helped him not to think too much. Because you can't forget, it was only a good six months earlier that he'd quit the force, and that's a situation where you've got to make your peace with it first.

And so the months in Zell helped him, of course. The coincidence that there was work for him here right away. But it couldn't go on like that forever, and now it was over.

And how I should put it, maybe the story with Nemec played a part, too, in why he was so downtrodden now. That it wasn't him who solved the case but Nemec. In other words, basically six months for nothing.

Never mind. The carpet pattern, it was a floral motif, but more like cogs, so if you can imagine: interlocking flowers. And if you looked at them long enough, you'd have thought they were turning.

Or maybe he was so depressed because, after all, it was a human tragedy. And suddenly it became clear to him. Lorenz. Vergolder. It came as a surprise, why now all of the sudden, why didn't it become clear to him earlier. But that's people for you, all of the sudden it becomes clear to you, and you yourself don't know why.

A few days ago he'd sat with Lorenz for hours and he'd talked to Vergolder. And now there wasn't even enough of them left for a proper burial.

The carpet was a color you almost can't describe, like honey that's gone hard. And the rotating flowers were basically the same color—in the light of day you couldn't really see them. But they popped out under artificial light.

But that wasn't it, because Brenner hadn't turned any lights on—to do that he would've had to move. It was already dusk, and Brenner wasn't quite sure whether he was still seeing the flowers or if they were only turning in his head.

The murdered Americans went through his head. What he'd read about them in Clare's composition for school, it was all coming back up. He was even feeling sorry for the glow-in-the-dark dial painters now, even though they wouldn't have been alive today anyway. And the forced laborers who froze to death, or fell to their deaths, building the dam.

Isn't that just how it is these days, when you're down in the dumps, then everything hits you all at once, and only the worst of it, of course. And that's what was going on with Brenner now, all these images surfacing one after another, perpetually slow and sticky, but none of them would disappear again. And all of them churning together, so slow, so viscous, that you've got to picture it like a washing machine, except, instead of water, it's honey.

Even Erni the waitress and her balcony were churning in the honey-washing-machine. And Andi the Fox looked so sad from the honey-washing-machine that Brenner thought: That's it, I'm getting up and turning the light on. Because by now it was completely dark. But Brenner could still see the flowers turning on the carpet. And next to Andi the Fox in the honey-washing-machine, the handless German was standing there and looking at Brenner through those centimeter-thick bifocals of hers.

Now, pay attention. It was seven-thirty. When Brenner finally went down to the bar in the Hirschenwirt. But he didn't take a seat. He just wanted a pack of cigarettes. Then, he went out to the street and smoked his first cigarette in eight months.

Now, as anybody who's quit smoking more than once knows. The first didn't taste good to him at all, more like horrible. Then, the second and the third usually taste like they used to. But the third still didn't taste good to Brenner. So he gave up and went back up to his room and went to sleep.

As he was falling asleep, he still found it surprising that the whole time he was smoking those three cigarettes, not a single person passed by on the street. Not a car, not a nothing. Needless to say, maybe he was just asleep already and it only seemed that way, i.e. dream-deserted.

It was eleven when he woke up. Now, you should know, whenever Brenner slept more than eight hours, he woke up with a headache. But now he'd slept fourteen hours. And right about the time he wants a doctor to saw his skull off with an electric compass saw, he wakes up. Needless to say, straight to the bathroom to puke, but the headache was only more severe afterward. You'd like to believe you can puke it out but not so.

At first he just wondered why his alarm had been going off for several minutes. Because he hadn't set it. And it was only once it'd stopped ringing that he realized that it was the telephone.

As he was finally getting into the shower, it rang again. Now for on-the-one-hand, on-the-other-hand. On the one hand, he didn't want to be dumb and, just because the phone's ringing, turn off the shower. Because, it goes without saying, nothing better to help you not feel a neck full of concrete—there's only warm water and nothing else. On the other hand, though, the telephone was making the exact same sound as the doctor's compass saw—okay, it'd have to be more of a ringing compass saw.

Needless to say, cutting off his head would've been the best thing right now, the only thing that actually helps when you've got a full-blown migraine like this. Showering just doesn't compare, compared to cutting your head off. But cutting off your head is one thing, and the sound of the compass saw is another thing altogether, because the ringing was driving Brenner crazy now. And he ran out of the shower without drying off and picked up the compass saw.

"Well, I'll be damned, look who's got a voice today!" the compass saw bawled.

That's interesting, though. Before Brenner even recognized Goggenberger the cabbie's voice, he already had the stench of Virginias in his nose. Now, of course, Brenner thought he was going to puke again, but then he said:

"Hm."

"You!"

"Hm?" Brenner says, because he was still having a problem with his voice.

"So yesterday I make six trips to the cemetery, yesterday I did. Six times, one day, cemetery, I'll be damned. But then they were burying Lorenz, didn't they?"

"Mm," Brenner says.

"I only ask because I wasn't there. I wanted to, but I'll be damned, a two-parter, no can do. I took a ride up to the funeral, and there I'm thinking to myself, this is convenient, you can stay right here, then, and go on in yourself. But on the drive there, another trip comes over the radio, and then another trip and another trip and another trip and another trip and another trip and another trip."

"Hm," Brenner tosses in, as if he wanted to say, but that makes seven trips already.

"That's why I wasn't there. Took today off, because I'm my own boss. Drove over to Kaprun, to the Seewirt. Ate goulash."

"Hm!" Ate goulash! Needless to say, that stirred Brenner's nausea all over again.

"The owner's a friend. Because I drive over there at least once a week to eat goulash."

Brenner wanted to hang up already, because the telephone cord wasn't long enough, let's say, for him to simultaneously be on the phone and puke into the toilet. So he still heard the cabbie when he said:

"I ask the owner, well, I'll be damned, why are you as pale as puked up *Griesskoch* today?"

"Hm."

"So the owner says, because I've got a dead body lying upstairs in one of my rooms. Who is it, I ask the owner, but, don't know him. I should take a good look at him, she says. I'll be damned, who do you think the dead guy was?"

"Hm?"

"Yeah, believe it or not, Lorenz!"

"I'll be damned."

Those were Brenner's first words all day. Now, you should know, for the migraines, he had pills that were so strong—I'm talking real bombers—that normally a single one made his stomach flip. But now he popped three right out of the package and swallowed them whole, no water.

Then he got dressed and went to what, at the Hirschenwirt, is called the lift. When he read the word "lift" above the lift, he thought of the corpses in the lift. That was, of course, a ski lift, not an elevator lift, but what can I say. Brenner took the stairs now anyhow, nice and slow, one step at a time, you'd have thought: rehab center.

The pink Chevrolet was parked right out front of the Hirschenwirt. When Brenner opened the car door, of course, immediately the bestial Virginia stench. Nothing, though, Brenner did not puke in Johnny's Chevrolet.

He let himself drop onto the passenger seat, and the cabbie peeled out. Needless to say, just as slow as ever. But Brenner was downright grateful for that now. He says:

"You're sure it's Lorenz?"

But Johnny just smiled, sure of victory. Just under half an hour he needed for the fifteen-kilometer county road, then he parked right in front of the inn. It may have been called the Seewirt, but it looked more like a run-down liquor store.

It was eleven-thirty. Brenner was just glad to be finally getting out of that stinking Chevrolet. The air in the parking lot seemed marvelous to him, a marvelous mountain air, because the Seewirt was pretty high up, 1,500 meters is where it was, and right behind it, the forest. Before he went any further, Brenner paused and took a few deep breaths.

Needless to say, all the worse when he opened the door to the inn. Because in the kitchen they were heating up grease again. Rancid, Brenner thought, and took a look around the bar at the inn. But not a soul was sitting there at this hour. Even before Brenner and the cabbie could take a seat themselves, hasty footsteps came coming down the hall. The kind of footsteps like when a woman in slippers goes scuffling over a stone floor. Apart from the slippers the woman had on a white smock that she probably only washed on Saturdays. And like I said, it was Friday.

She didn't even ask if the two of them wanted something to drink now, no, had to tell her whole story right away. Because, needless to say, she was afraid that she might be suspected of something. She stood there at the foot of their table and looked at Brenner anxiously the whole time she was talking.

"We close at midnight. But often, if nothing's going on, we close at ten or eleven, whenever the last guest leaves. Business isn't so good up here. Since my husband died, it's got worse every year. Only in the winter, because the skiers come in, is it halfway good. In summer, bad, and now, not at all. Just a few card players."

Now, you can't forget that Brenner hadn't had any breakfast, not even a cup of coffee. But he also didn't want to interrupt the woman, so he simply fished around in the bread basket on the sideboard, because right beside their table was the sideboard. The old dry slices of yesterday's bread were exactly what he needed right now.

"Yesterday, though, the card players stayed late, Fulterer, he's the assistant forester, and Brokal, the engineer from the power plant, and the bank director, and Fandl who owns the place down the road. Every Wednesday they're here and playing *tarock*. Normally from about eight to about ten, but this Wednesday there was a soccer game, so they watched it here, a couple others were here, too, because these days, everybody's got a TV, but some of them prefer to watch here at the bar.

When the game was over, the others left, and Brokal the engineer and Fulterer tried to leave, too. But the bank director wanted to play another hand, because he's retired and doesn't have to get up in the morning. And so they stayed.

At eleven, Leitinger came in, he was drunk and ordered himself another beer. Around eleven-thirty another car drove up. Then, in comes a man I've never seen before. He was so white in the face that I wanted to ask him what'll it be. And the card players were watching, too. But before I could even get around to it, he ordered himself a double schnapps and downed it. Then another double and another. Leitinger, drunk himself, says to him: You sure are thirsty.

But the stranger didn't seem to hear him at all. You'd have thought he didn't hear or see anything that was happening around him. Then, another double and downed it again. Just after midnight, the card players quit and wanted to leave. I cashed out their tabs, Leitinger's, too, and then I went over to the stranger and said we're closing now. So, he says he'll be on his way, but before he does, he'd like another bottle of rum. I'm thinking to myself, He wants it to go, the bottle of rum, that often happens that people show up here out of the blue because they forgot to go shopping, and buy a bottle of wine or a few beers to go.

The others said, too, that they didn't think he'd put the rum bottle right in his mouth and empty it in one fell swoop. Like it was water, you'd have thought. And not rum—eighty percent.

We're all standing around him now, and nobody says a word. In hindsight, though, I think we were all thinking more or less the same thing. But Leitinger was the only one to say it out loud, probably just because he himself was drunk.

At first we all stood there silent, even Leitinger, a whole 'nother minute at least, after the stranger drank the bottle of rum. It was three quarters of a liter of eighty percent. We just watched him and waited for him to fall over. But he didn't fall over. And so Leitinger said, I think he's a ghost.

Now, in the light of day, that sounds silly, but at the time, I was actually afraid that he might be, just because he didn't fall over. And it got more and more eerie, this man, the way he stood there next to his empty bottle of rum and didn't fall over. And then he asked me if we have rooms, too. Completely normal, not slurring his words. Completely normal, asked if we have rooms, too.

Yes, I said, we've got rooms, even though I was afraid, but, on the other hand, I was just glad that he said something at all.

At this point, the men left—they weren't feeling too good, either, you could tell from looking at them. And I showed the stranger upstairs to his room. He walked behind me, maybe a little unsteady on his feet, but not much, you only would've noticed it if you knew about it, but nothing tragic. I said good night, and he said good night, and then I went to sleep—and double-checked that I'd locked up behind me. I couldn't fall asleep at first, but since I didn't hear anything else out of the stranger, I fell asleep after all.

So, when he didn't stir right away in the morning, I wasn't exactly surprised. That he was sleeping the drink off. Wasn't a ghost after all, I thought to myself, if he's got to sleep one off, too. But, then, I did go look in on him. There he was, lying dead on the floor. Didn't even make it into bed."

Brenner didn't finish his bread now, but asked the owner if she'd show him the body. He followed her up the creaky wooden stairs to the second floor. And when the owner unlocked the door to the room, he no longer wondered if the dead man was really Lorenz.

"I just thought he was going to take the bottle of rum to go," the owner said.

"There, there," Brenner said. She was scared of the police, and that was convenient for him now, of course. Because he was going to need a few hours.

"Lock the room back up," he said, and then the two of them went back down the narrow wooden staircase, but he took the lead this time and the owner followed. Interesting, though. On the way down, the steps creaked much less than on the way up. The cabbie was waiting at the bottom, because, needless to say, him with his 120 kilos wasn't going back up those stairs anytime soon. But he got his moment of triumph now because Brenner hadn't believed him at first, this whole story about Lorenz.

"And don't talk to anybody about this. Above all, not

with the police. I'll be back this evening," Brenner says to the owner outside in the parking lot.

And sitting back in the taxi now, he asks Johnny: "Do you know where Andi the Fox lives?"

Johnny didn't say yes and he didn't say no, but Brenner knew him well enough by now to know that meant: "Yes."

"Why is it exactly that you drive so slow?"

"I drive perfectly normal."

Now, of course—Brenner still had his headache. And for every meter that Johnny crawled along, it seemed to him like his headache got twice as bad. He tapped on the glove box nervously with his fingers, it was made of wood in Johnny's old Chevrolet, but the tapping was no use, and so Brenner said:

"For god's sake, drive a little faster!"

"I'm not a fire truck," the cabbie said, pulling a half-smoked Virginia out of his jacket pocket and relighting it.

But Brenner knew that he only had a couple hours' time now, because if he wasn't back by evening, the owner would call the police anyhow, out of sheer fright.

"I'm telling you nicely for the last time now that you should drive faster!" Brenner shouted.

But Johnny Goggenberger the taxi driver only slowed down demonstrably. "And I'm telling you nicely for the last time now that my Chevy hasn't gone over seventy in twenty-three years and it's not going to today, either!"

Now, that was only half-true. Because, shortly thereafter, eyewitnesses saw the pink Chevrolet racing well over a hundred in the direction of Zell.

They were surprised, because Johnny's driving style was known near and far. And they couldn't have known that Brenner was sitting next to him and pointing his brand new Glock at the cabbie. Needless to say, Brenner was glad now that he'd popped by Perterer Jr.'s one more time after all the day before yesterday.

"Well, I'll be damned. You're going to be sorry," the agreeable chauffeur said.

"If you say 'I'll be damned' one more time, I'll shoot."

In his other hand Brenner had the car phone and was calling information to get Andi's number. But it was just his mother at home, and naturally: no clue where Andi was.

"New destination: Preussenstadl," Brenner says to Johnny, with the gun still in his hand. Within a matter of minutes, the Chevrolet was there.

"Look, that wasn't so bad now, was it, Johnny?" Brenner says and gets out.

"I'll be damned, you lunatic!" Johnny says and drives off so fast, you'd have thought he didn't realize that nobody was threatening him with a gun anymore.

CHAPTER 13

The Preussenstadl looked like a cabin, but not like the kind you're thinking: rustic. Because it had five floors with fifty-two apartments, I'm talking ultra-modern on the inside with two elevators. And so you never had to wait very long for the elevator to come, because when one of them's way up on the fifth floor, and you're waiting in the lobby, that's what the second elevator's for.

But Brenner didn't take the elevator now. Handless lived on the fourth floor, but somehow Brenner had something against elevators on this particular day, you can't forget: headache and then all the excitement, so maybe a person prefers to take the stairs instead of stepping into an elevator.

The German lived in an east-facing *garçonnière* on the fourth floor. She buzzed him in the front door to the Preussenstadl, practically the instant Brenner rang the bell. He was surprised that she didn't even ask who it was through the intercom, but just pressed the buzzer. Needless to say, though. He didn't know the entrance to the Preussenstadl was monitored by a surveillance camera. You'd like to think a detective would notice a thing like this, but he'd reckoned so little on there being a camera behind the antlers that he hadn't noticed it.

Now, when he got to the fourth floor, he saw right away that one of the apartment doors was ajar, practically, come in. He gave a light knock, though, more out of formality, and then he went in. He wasn't surprised, of course, to find that the German wasn't alone now. Because he'd come here on account of Andi, and so it didn't surprise him that Andi was there, either. But he wasn't expecting to find that, in addition to Andi and the German, somebody else was there. And Andi was already looking scared, but Clare Corrigan, so pale—white doesn't come close.

It couldn't have been the light, though, because the German looked perfectly normal, and when you consider, an old woman, she even looked flat-out healthy.

Now, the German had a glass coffee table in her living room, and the three were sitting around it and watching as Brenner walked into the apartment. Because the door between the foyer and the living room was standing wide open. The foyer had gray laminate flooring and the living room had been laid in fleecy white carpet. It struck Brenner all over again that the camera he didn't notice but the carpet he does.

"You can keep your shoes on," the German says.

Because she'd noticed his hesitation, of course. On the one hand, he was reluctant, street shoes on white carpet. But on the other hand. Entering the living room in socks— at that moment it seemed like the entrance to the Heidnische Kirche.

"Please have a seat!" the German says, genially, after he takes a few timid steps across the white carpet, and it was so soft that you really sank into it.

Now, surrounding the glass coffee table was an honest-to-goodness sectional, so, plenty of room. On one section sat the German, and next to her was Andi, so they were facing the door that Brenner came in through. Clare was sitting with her back to the window, because, across from the window, the TV was on with the sound off. Briefly he wondered how Clare would react if he were to sit directly across from her so that she couldn't see the TV. But then he said:

"I prefer to stand."

"Would you care for something to drink?"

The migraine pills always made him terribly thirsty, he'd often drink five, six liters of water in a day. And today, three pills and practically no water, so you can imagine just how thirsty he was.

"No thanks, not thirsty."

The German got a little irritated now, in a way that Brenner had never cared for.

"Do sit down!"

He just couldn't stand this tone. When somebody got snippy with him. And especially when it's an old woman, he was particularly sensitive. Psychological, maybe.

Adults used to always take this righteous tone when they were saying something about your hair, back when Brenner still had long hair, i.e. the sixties. He was briefly reminded of this understated aggression now. That it's just not natural for you not to go to the barber.

That was a long time ago. Over twenty years ago he'd cut it. At first people didn't recognize him. Even his best friends were startled a second before they were able to tell who he was.

"I prefer to stand."

"As you wish. Why are you—to what do I owe the honor? Can I help you in some way?"

"It's not you that I'm here about, actually."

Now Brenner looks at Andi, next to the German, and says:

"I'm sorry. But Lorenz is dead."

Needless to say, now, the German, biblical wrath:

"Are you trying to torment us? Two days after the funeral you're making jokes about it?"

Because she couldn't have known. But Andi, of course, you almost couldn't see him anymore, he'd sank so deep into the couch. Because the sectional was beige, and so was Andi now—so beige that he almost blended into the sectional. Just his aqua-blue eyes stared out from the sectional, all the more scared.

Czech eyes, Brenner thought, and said:

"Last night Lorenz turned up at a pub in Kaprun. Poisoned himself with a bottle of rum. And early this morning the owner found him dead."

But the German refused to believe it:

"And who identified him?"

"I did," Brenner says.

"In what pub, then?" the German says. But not quite as resolute now.

"Actually I wanted to ask you something," Brenner says.

Andi just nodded in silence. Because, needless to say, Andi knew what was coming.

"Would you prefer to talk in private?" Brenner says.

No, Andi indicated.

"You told everybody that Lorenz died in the fire with Vergolder. Even though you saw with your own eyes that Lorenz got away."

Brenner looked Andi in the eyes. Well, the two light-blue studs that were spaced a few centimeters apart and riveted to the beige back of the couch. From his eyes, you couldn't have detected the slightest sign that Andi was about to say something. But all of the sudden he says:

"Lorenz ran down to the lake with me. I said, we'll make it out to be an accident. Or better yet, it was! Vergolder's the guilty one, I say to Lorenz. If he gasses up with a cigarette in his mouth. Everybody will see it like that, I say. The police, the insurance, everybody will see it like that, I say. We just have to give the same exact statement, I say to Lorenz. That Vergolder—"

As Andi fell silent, Brenner didn't think he'd say another word. Because he believed he was dissolving into the sectional with each passing moment, and only the glassy studs in the beige couch-back would be left. But then Andi said:

"Lorenz didn't want to know anything about it. He shouted at me that on no condition was I to say it was an accident. Because everybody absolutely needed to know that he'd had it with Vergolder. Officially had it. Just like my boss always yells when a customer pisses him off: I've had it with you. Lorenz yelled, I have to tell everybody that he's officially had it with his uncle."

"So why didn't you do it?"

"But I did, right from the start! I told everybody that Lorenz had done it on purpose."

Andi sits up so straight on the sectional now, you'd have thought he felt the need to justify to Lorenz, not Brenner, why he'd given a false statement.

"And that Lorenz died in the fire? Did you come up with that one, too?"

"It's not a shame about Vergolder. It is a shame about Lorenz."

That was the German there, chiming in again now. She'd taken her thick glasses off and was rubbing her eyes with her arm-stumps. Because, needless to say, she wants to rub her eyes just as much as the next person when she's tired. But people are often weird about things like this, and it was uncomfortable for Brenner to watch her do it.

Five, six times in a row she made the exact same movement. With her right arm-stump, vigorously across the forehead and then down along the outer edge of the nose and around the eye—you'd have thought she was trying to press her eyeball right into her skull. Then, across the forehead again and over to the other eye.

Like I said, it made Brenner uncomfortable, but in spite of this, he found it impossible to look away. Now, pay attention, because it wasn't because of the arm movements, okay, arm-stumps—no, it was because of the German's eyes. For the first time, he truly saw her eyes, because normally they were always magnified and distorted humongously big by the thick bifocals, like a fish, you'd have thought, or how you sometimes see in a nature museum, sort of like an extinct animal.

Needless to say, the German had much smaller eyes in reality. But it wasn't that. Something else about her eyes was bothering Brenner. But now he's thinking, Maybe it's just the liveliness of hers compared to the glassiness of Andi's doll-eyes.

Then she put her glasses back on, and softly she said:

"It's so typical of all of you. Blaming the Americans' murder on Lorenz."

"That's how the police see it anyway."

"And how do you see it?"

"Well, how do you see it?" Brenner asks. But he was thinking about something else completely. Or better put, not thinking. You've got to picture it like when there's a word on the tip of your tongue. And it just doesn't come to you, even though you can feel it there on your tongue. Except that it wasn't a word that Brenner was searching for.

Now, easier said, of course, like people always say: Don't think about it and it'll come to you. Because how are you supposed to not think about it when you absolutely want to know it. And that's exactly what was going on with Brenner, he couldn't do anything else but stare intently through the thick bifocal lenses and into the eyes of the German.

But not what you're thinking, that it was something weird that had him so preoccupied. No, something familiar is what it was. It had him feeling, how should I put it, uneasy. Or should I say: scared. But these weren't the words that he was looking for on the tip of his tongue now. I mean, practically speaking, it wasn't his tongue at all where he was looking. Not on the tip of his tongue, but in the eyes, as it were, because it was an image that he was searching for this whole time. What kind of image, though? Don't think about it, don't think about it.

"Vergolder," the German says. Because that was her answer to his question, of course, who, in her opinion, killed the Americans. But that was just the same old story and Brenner wasn't the least bit interested in hearing it now.

But pay attention. Because for one whole second, well, maybe it's just like with downhill skiing, when the victor wins by a thousandth of a second. So for only a thousandth of a second, the detective thought of something else altogether now.

How he took the subway for the first time. He was eighteen at the time, went to London after his high school graduation. And when you're waiting there on the platform, you know, here comes the train, before you even see it or hear it. Because you feel the draft from the station before yours, because the train's practically ramming an air cushion.

"Say that again," Brenner says.

"Vergolder," the German says again.

"I have a favor to ask," the detective says.

"If I can be of help to you," the German says, and even smiled as she did so.

"Would you mind taking your glasses off again?"

Now, it wouldn't have been conspicuous in and of itself

for the old woman to have so many wrinkles around her eyes. But this was a real aureole. And it reminded Brenner of the millions of fine crows' feet that, in old age, his Aunt Klara had got on her upper lip.

She'd stubbornly insisted to everybody that it was from smoking, because she'd been a heavy smoker, and she imagined, when you take a drag on a cigarette, these concertina folds form on your upper lip. But, then, her half-sister got the exact same wrinkles in old age, too, and that was Brenner's mother, and her whole life long she never smoked.

And Brenner says to Handless now:

"I always thought it was from the eye surgery. Your brother's eyes were always so squinty like he was looking at the sun. And millions of crow's feet around the eyes. I automatically thought it was from the surgery."

"No, no, it's not because of the surgery," Vergolder's sister said, completely calm now, "it runs in our family. Our mother also had a kind of wreath around her eyes, not just in old age—started when she was forty. A leathery, wrinkly skin, like a dried-up leather apple. Are you familiar with leather apples?"

"Fifty years after you disappeared from Zell, you return. Only to take revenge on your brother."

Brenner even surprised himself when his voice trembled there. As if he was afraid that the obvious similarity between Handless and her brother, Vergolder, might suddenly dissolve.

"Leather apples have a thick, leathery skin. Often people call them cooking apples, because you cook them and use them for apple sauce. Or for apple strudel. But if you peel them, they taste good raw, too."

"Weren't you worried that somebody in Zell would recognize you again?"

Now Handless got up and went over to the TV. Above the TV was a bookshelf, and on it was a small picture frame.

Now, maybe you're familiar with this, when you go to an old person's apartment, hanging all over the place are these ancient black-and-white photos: the grandfather of the grandfather, from the First World War or even earlier, or these retouched portraits that make you think, centuries old.

"That's what I looked like, you see, when they chased me away. Do you see any similarity?"

Brenner didn't know what he should say. But Handless sure knew what to say:

"Nobody in Zell would've recognized me, even if I weren't fifty years older and fifty kilos heavier. Even if I looked exactly like I did back then, still not a soul would've recognized me again. Forgetting is a kind of mercy, you have to know that. And God showed mercy upon the Zellers—in spades."

"And your own brother? You had to run into him."

"Like I said: mercy."

"But you know no mercy. That community theater of yours—you didn't perform in a theater."

"No, but we did perform in the community," Vergolder's sister says, as if she were saying the most normal thing in the world.

"And you put it on with real people. Lorenz and Clare

and Andi were your marionettes. They didn't realize at all that you'd been playing out your own drama with them for some time. That you only needed a couple of dummies that could be useful—that could be turned against Vergolder, easy."

"At first I only wanted to mess with him a little. I gave Elfi the book about the dial painters to read. Very interesting. She identified quite strongly by then with Clare Corrigan, the dial painter who died. And then the idea with the community theater. Lorenz and Andi were completely wild about the idea of sticking it to Vergolder."

"At the theater. Except that you actually approached Vergolder's stepfather."

"No, no, it was the American who approached me."

Brenner didn't understand how he was making it rain just now, I mean, why now, you've got to picture it like an ATM that suddenly starts spitting out coins. Like his brain was spitting out explanations all at once now, after being here three-quarters of a year for nothing. Well, isn't this just the way it always goes for me, Brenner thought. Now, where it's too late, where Handless's eyes have told me everything anyhow, it's now that I notice the things that somebody else would've noticed much sooner.

But he was being unfair to himself there. Because, who knows if he would've noticed that bit about the eyes if he didn't already have the other things somewhere in the back of his mind? And he says to Handless now:

"I thought as much: the binoculars that the American bought from Perterer Jr., they couldn't be the whole surprise for their sixtieth anniversary. And even before then I thought, there's just no two ways about it, they must've got on the lift willingly."

In three-quarters of a year, though, you get to thinking quite a bit. And he himself wasn't even certain now if he'd come up with the bit about the *Vormachen*. It seemed to him as if it'd been going around in his head the whole time. He knew that the Americans had met while skiing. Now, of course, he could make sense of it quite easily:

"The American buys the binoculars because, for their anniversary, he wants to give his wife a nighttime *Vormachen* in the ski lift. He commissions you to perform with your would-be theater group. And in order for the two of them to be able to sit next to each other in a single-chair lift, she gets on at the top and him at the bottom so that they can meet in the middle. Except that you and your *Vormachen* group don't show up. No, the two eighty-year-olds are left sitting in their box seats, twenty meters in the air."

But Handless, now, quite insistent:

"Lorenz, Clare, and Andi didn't do anything. I persuaded the American that it would be the greatest show if his wife rode the lift down and watched through the binoculars as he rode up to her. And the moment they were at a certain height, the lift would stay put. As if by magic."

"And then it just sat there, the lift. And then you really didn't do anything, either."

"Nothing at all," Handless smiled.

Now, end of September, almost thirty degrees Celsius. Brenner gets a slight chill. The question momentarily escapes him, why the Americans of all people got the kiss of death. Why not the despised brother himself. There are these moments, though, where things occur to you that don't otherwise occur to you over the course of weeks and months, not until now, at these moments. And now Brenner says:

"That's why the Americans were so excited about this *Vormachen*, because they'd liked it so much back then, after the war, at their daughter's wedding to Vergolder. You told me that Vergolder had been offended at the time. Because of the story with the nurse. But this nurse that the *Vormachen* had hinted at—"

"—wasn't a nurse at all, of course. But just a sister," Vergolder's sister finished, perfectly calm now. And then she said:

"The Americans had impressed upon me: it has to be every bit as amusing as the story about the sister was back then. And how else was I supposed to make it every bit as amusing?"

Needless to say, Brenner was glad that he wasn't expected to give an answer now. Vergolder's handless sister sat back down on the couch again. She set the photo on the glass coffee table in front of her and looked at it so intently that you'd have thought she was seeing it for the first time.

"Have you ever noticed how many melancholiacs there are in Zell? In nearly every family, there's either an imbecile or a melancholiac. And more often than not, both."

People often say, I'm shocked, but it goes without saying, they're just saying that, and really they only mean that something's come as a shock to them, no talk of actual shocking. But if the doctor were to place a couple of electrodes on the side of your head and give you a dose of electricity, that's roughly how Brenner felt right now. As Vergolder's handless sister suddenly dispensed with her perfect High German. And instead lapsed into her obsolete dialect, full of old-fashioned words:

"Loads of melancholiacs."

The word itself was making Brenner a bit melancholy.

"And loads of imbeciles. Too many mountains, the valleys all too narrow, villages too small. When I got pregnant, I went to the priest. A nice priest, Father Reiter. He said: Zell has always been a den of incest."

"Lorenz, that was your child. And your brother, Vergolder, was Lorenz's father."

"I wouldn't have named him Lorenz. By the time of the baptism, though, they'd already got rid of me."

"But they used to baptize the children right away back then, within just a few days of the birth."

"They'd already got rid of me."

"And you never saw your child again?"

"Not until a year and a half ago, when I returned to Zell. Then I got to know him."

"And then you told him your story and he couldn't cope with it and put three people in their graves."

"I didn't tell him anything. Just got to know him, but told him nothing. Lorenz didn't know anything. And he didn't kill anybody, either."

"Except his father."

"That used to be completely normal."

"Lighting your father on fire?"

"The only thing that wasn't normal was my love for my brother. Him getting me pregnant, maybe that didn't used to be normal exactly, either, but it happened often enough. But me, of course. I had to go and love him. He was twenty-four, and I was seventeen. Needless to say, young. I just had to love him. Around the time I got pregnant, he met that American. Once the child was born, they took it away from me. Another brother who was already married. He took it. So, I had to leave. Home from the hospital and gone in the night. Because I had to have the child at the hospital—bring no disgrace on the home. The people believed I left because I'd brought home an illegitimate child. Believed I walked into the lake. But I didn't walk into the lake. I went to Germany to be a waitress. It wasn't much better. I lay down on the train tracks. But, then, at the last moment. Only, my hands, I was too slow."

"And after fifty years you came back and got your son to kill his father."

"He didn't even know that he was his father. Or me, his mother."

"But the hatred that you drummed into him was enough to—"

"—he had his own reasons for hating him. Every year, a passbook. Otherwise, nothing but contempt. I didn't have to talk Lorenz into anything. We always had an unspoken bond. Mother and son. It all came about on its own."

"And the checks just falsified themselves?"

"That was just foolish of Lorenz. He went and signed the checks instead of coming to me when he needed money."

"And Elfi stole them for him up at Vergolder's castle. Just like she did with the keys to the lift for you."

"It's Clare," Clare said.

That was all of it. Then, nobody said anything else. All four sat there in silence, and the TV played on with the sound off. And just as Brenner had collected himself, just as he was about to ask that one last question, it was already too late. A cruel buzzing startled them, prodding them out of their lethargy. And the person doing the buzzing didn't take his finger off the buzzer until Handless buzzed him in.

A moment later two police officers stormed in: Kollarik in the lead, Hochreiter taking up the rear. And weren't even all the way in the apartment yet before Kollarik started shouting his head off. Like that even works—that you can shout your one and only head off, over and over again. Because Kollarik, the Zellers always called him "Choleric."

Now, what was he shouting at Brenner for. Brenner only understood as much as Goggenberger the cabbie had tipped him off to. Now, Hochreiter had one less star on his uniform than Kollarik did. But while Kollarik was still blowing his top, Brenner put a word in police inspector Hochreiter's ear.

Hochreiter's skin was so red, you could tell right away: sailing or glacier skiing. Nevertheless, though. With each word from Brenner, his face just got redder. And then, needless to say, the contrast with the blue uniform. Kollarik even quit shouting when he saw Hochreiter turn red.

Then, it went fast. Because these kinds of things, at first

they take months and years, and then, once it gets to a certain point, it goes so fast that you almost miss it.

Because Handless made no effort to deny anything. And Hochreiter says—interesting, though, the degree of respect in his voice:

"Hopefully, you are aware, Frau Antretter, that we're going to have to take you in."

And that, of course, that was Kollarik's moment. He'd been so furious that he'd only made himself look ridiculous with all his shouting anyway. "Take you in," though, that was his cue. You couldn't have looked fast enough, already there in front of Vergolder's sister with the handcuffs out.

But Handless just made an embarrassed gesture and, pityingly, said:

"Now you don't know where you're supposed to put the handcuffs on me."

CHAPTER 14

When Brenner unlocked the door to his civil service apartment, it felt like he'd truly been away for three-quarters of a year. Even though he had, in fact, come back now and then just to check that everything was copacetic.

Somehow sentimental, though, because Zell, *finito,* and what's to become of Brenner now. One thing you can't forget, a sheer stroke of luck that he even got the job, and just as he was leaving the force, too.

Still one thing to do, though. Because he still had to write that report for the Meierling Detective Agency, once and for all. And because he knew for a fact, If I don't write it now, I never will, he fixed himself a cup of coffee. Popped a quick pill, because the first one he'd taken on the train hadn't done anything at all. But then, pronto, the typewriter, unpacked, time to hop to it.

But just as he was typing the date, the phone rang. *Now, should I get it, or should I not get it,* but it wouldn't stop ringing, so he gets it:

"Yeah, Brenner here."

"Brennero! A real honor."

"I'm sorry, you have the wrong number, this is the automated answering machine."

"So modest! You can afford it! This is the automated questioning machine, Monsieur Mandl!"

"Unfortunately I share a line with three other people, Mandl. The neighbors will be wanting to make a phone call."

"You can't hook up an answering machine to a party line. Why, this wouldn't be Brenner himself speaking, would it?"

"What do you want, Mandl?"

"Interview with the cunning secret agent."

"Talk to Nemec, he likes that kind of thing."

"That's an obstruction of my work, Brenner. And if you go on the dole now, who's going to pay your unemployment if I'm not working?"

"I'm not going on the dole."

"The next case awaits our cunning secret agent! That's something even our last reader can accept."

"No next case."

"Top-secret, though, he's not allowed to speak about it! Our last reader will have complete sympathy!"

"Listen, Mandl, either talk like a normal person—"

"Or you tell me how you figured it out."

"Figured what out, Mandl?"

"How the German with no hands on her is Vergolder's sister."

"That was your job, Mandl."

"Hey, that doesn't surprise me one bit now."

"When the forged checks turned up, the ones that Lorenz signed with the names of both Parsons."

"When it came to drawing, one of a kind talent, Lorenz. So a signature's nothing."

"And surely you remember the headline of your article, too."

"When it comes to writing, one of a kind talent, Mandl. One of a kind! But you're going to have to jog my memory on this one now."

"Resurrection of the Dead."

"Yeah, yeah, even though it wasn't even Easter."

"What did you actually mean by that at the time?"

"Well, if the Parsons were issuing checks after their deaths. For all intents and purposes, they'd have to be resurrected. It was no different for Jesus, either."

"So, plural: the dead. Possessive: of the dead."

"Yeah, say, Brenner!"

"But for Jesus, it'd be singular: Resurrection of the dead."

"Yeah, say, Brenner, what are you asking me all this for?"

"For what, Mandl, it's: for what are you asking me all this. And what is it when Vergolder's sister is resurrected?"

"It's—aha! Yet again, Resurrection of the dead."

"Exactly. Because that's what we've got uncountable nouns for."

"'The Grammar Gumshoe!' Our last reader will be proud of you, Brenner. And the dead, resurrected after fifty years, just so she could bring two others to their deaths. Rather un-Christian, so far as resurrection goes."

"Maybe she just wanted to make her brother nervous."

"'Paranormal Trickery!' Didn't pull it off, though. She turns back up after fifty years, but the Zellers simply aren't scared. Ghost completely forgotten. Had to stir things up a little in Zell. Get some stories buzzing around. Get people excited about the Heidnische Kirche."

"But you guys still weren't scared."

"Exactly, we don't scare that easy. So, the ghost had to stir things up a little more."

"But you guys still weren't scared. Exactly, Mandl."

"But we were! Me and my reader, we were scared that there were dead people hopping the ski lift."

"But only because they didn't have a day pass."

"Eh, Brenner, what good's a day pass at night. But one thing you still have to explain to me. Why did the ghost go to such lengths? Normally, a ghost like that would just get a revolver. Not a ski lift, though."

"Except the ghost didn't have any hands."

"Logical, except the ghost didn't have any hands. So, better off with the big, blunt lever on the lift."

"That's it, Mandl."

"But how does a ghost like that get you to sit on a ski lift all night? How does she lure you there?"

"Very simple."

Brenner hadn't quite noticed. In his left hand, he was holding the receiver, but his right index finger, well, it was like it had a will of its own. Simply pressed the button on the cradle and away with Mandl.

It has to be said, Mandl simply had no knack for journalism. Every detail interested him. But how Lorenz got rubbed out by his own parents, Vergolder and Vergolder's sister, one more brutal than the next. Mandl would've made a tragedy out of it, practically Greek. But, no.

Now, maybe telepathy does exist or something, because at that moment, where Brenner's thinking, A pity about Kati Engljähringer, and maybe I'll try giving her another call, I've got the time now—the phone rings again, and needless to say, Mandl again:

"Antretter's sister told the police that it was Lorenz who orchestrated the keys to the lift and the checks from his uncle's."

"Must've been," Brenner says.

Because Elfi, she now had a dead father who'd never even officially been her father. And she'd dropped out of school. And her job, of course, you can scratch that, too. And Lorenz, dead. And the only person who'd ever took any care of her, in prison. And Brenner thought, Elfi's stuck in Zell, and that's punishment enough. But Mandl says:

"Now, I've got a freshly typed article lying here that'll make Mandl famous. Because he uncovers that Elfi must've been responsible for the keys to the lift. Besides which, she helped the old American into the chair lift up at the terminal station, while Handless was waiting down at the valley station with the other American."

"How are you able to shave when you're constantly retching into the mirror?"

"Electric, Brenner. With the Phili-shaver. I'm a pro at shaving. But good ol' Mandl's got a little deal to strike with you now. A deal, Brenner."

"A deal for who?"

"For little Elfi Lohninger, alias Clare Corrigan, a deal. Because I'm just going to put this article in my drawer for now. And that's where it'll stay. Until the moment where you get the big idea of calling—or in any other way contacting— the lovely schoolteacher, Frau Kati Engljähringer."

"You're a real mensch, Mandl. Then, please give my regards to Engljähringer, unless that falls under 'contact,' too."

The report, now. These things don't just happen right away, Brenner thought, and it was only six-thirty. And maybe before I get started I'll take a Migradon. Because, needless to say, talking on the phone only made his headache worse.

First he goes to the mailbox, maybe some welcome news. But only a letter from the Civil Service Housing Authority. It looked so official that Brenner thought better of opening it up today.

Now, the report. He would've preferred hitting the sack, even though it was only just after six-thirty. Because three Migradons, and not the slightest effect. But, no wonder, because people would remember this year for a long time to come.

Now, one thing you can't forget. It was already the twenty-fifth of September. And still twenty-seven degrees Celsius. And believe it or not. Thirteen hours later, Brenner would be woken up by the sound of the snowplows.